Contents

CHIBA

TRANS-CHIBA
ULTRA QUIZ

MY YOUTH R♥MANTIC C☺MEDY iS WRØNG, AS I EXPECTED

Wataru Watari
Illustration **Ponkan⑧**

VOLUME

7.5

YEN
ON

NEW YORK

MY YOUTH ROMANTIC COMEDY IS WRONG, AS I EXPECTED Vol. 7.5
WATARU WATARI
Illustration by Ponkan⑧

Translation by Jennifer Ward
Cover art by Ponkan⑧

YAHARI ORE NO SEISHUN LOVE COME WA MACHIGATTEIRU.
Vol. 7.5 by Wataru WATARI
© 2011 Wataru WATARI
Illustration by PONKAN⑧
All rights reserved.
Original Japanese edition published by SHOGAKUKAN.
English translation rights in the United States of America, Canada, the United Kingdom, Ireland, Australia and New Zealand arranged with SHOGAKUKAN through Tuttle-Mori Agency, Inc.

English translation © 2019 by Yen Press, LLC

Yen On
1290 Avenue of the Americas
New York, NY 10104

Visit us at yenpress.com
facebook.com/yenpress
twitter.com/yenpress
yenpress.tumblr.com
instagram.com/yenpress

First Yen On Edition: June 2019

Yen On is an imprint of Yen Press, LLC.
The Yen On name and logo are trademarks of Yen Press, LLC.

Library of Congress Cataloging-in-Publication Data
Names: Watari, Wataru, author. | Ponkan 8, illustrator.
Title: My youth romantic comedy is wrong, as I expected / Wataru Watari ; illustration by Ponkan 8.
Other titles: Yahari ore no seishun love come wa machigatteiru. English
Description: New York : Yen On, 2016–
Identifiers: LCCN 2016005816 | ISBN 9780316312295 (v. 1 : pbk.) | ISBN 9780316396011 (v. 2 : pbk.) |
    ISBN 9780316318068 (v. 3 : pbk.) | ISBN 9780316318075 (v. 4 : pbk.) | ISBN 9780316318082 (v. 5 : pbk.) |
    ISBN 9780316411868 (v. 6 : pbk.) | ISBN 9781975384128 (v. 7 : pbk.) | ISBN 9781975384159 (v. 7.5 : pbk.)
Subjects: | CYAC: Optimism—Fiction. | School—Fiction.
Classification: LCC PZ7.1.W396 My 2016 | DDC [Fic]—dc23
LC record available at http://lccn.loc.gov/2016005816

ISBN: 978-1-9753-8415-9

10 9 8 7 6 5 4 3 2 1

LSC-C

Printed in the United States of America

MY YOUTH
R♥MANTIC
C☻MEDY iS
WRØNG, AS
I EXPECTED

seven and
a half

Cast of Characters

Hachiman Hikigaya .... The main character. High school second-year. Twisted personality.

Yukino Yukinoshita .... Captain of the Service Club. Perfectionist.

Yui Yuigahama .... Hachiman's classmate. Tends to worry about what other people think.

Yoshiteru Zaimokuza .... Nerd. Ambition is to become a light-novel author.

Saika Totsuka .... In tennis club. Very cute. A boy, though.

Saki Kawasaki .... Hachiman's classmate. Sort of a delinquent type.

Hayato Hayama .... Hachiman's classmate. Popular. In the soccer club.

Kakeru Tobe .... Hachiman's classmate. An excitable character and member of Hayama's clique.

Yumiko Miura .... Hachiman's classmate. Reigns over the girls in class as queen bee.

Hina Ebina .... Hachiman's classmate. Part of Miura's clique, but a slash fangirl.

Shizuka Hiratsuka .... Japanese teacher. Guidance counselor.

Haruno Yukinoshita .... Yukino's older sister. In university.

Komachi Hikigaya .... Hachiman's little sister. In her third year in middle school.

Yui's Diary

Sablé

6 June

★ Birthday ★
18

"Komachi Hikigaya's Plot."
BT 063

Love,
Sablé

7 July

3 Final exams start!
↓

SAB **They** have yet to know of a place they should go back to.
107

13 Event \(^ー^)/
14 Hina's birthday 🐟

20 Summer vacation!!!!!!!!!!
↓

8 August

1 Service Club camp ☆☆
↓ (until the 3rd)

8 Hikki's birthday

11 Family trip ☺
↓ (until the 1?

17 Fireworks fes

2 **F**

YUI ☆

9 September

10 October

11 November

10 Athletic festival‼️‼️‼️

12 School field trip! 😃
Kyoto!! (till the 15th) ↓

14 Cultural festival
15

21 ✉ Respond to e-mails! ↓

27 Staying over at Yukinon's place

SS 1 — Hachiman Hikigaya's idea of "Mom's cooking" is wrong, as I expected. 005

Short Story 1
Hachiman Hikigaya's idea of "Mom's cooking" is wrong, as I expected.

It was the height of fall, the season of reading. Normally, I would be deep in a book right about then, but that day it would not be so. Instead, we were having a staring contest with the laptop Miss Hiratsuka had shoved in our faces.

"'The Chiba Prefecture–Wide Advice E-mail…'" I repeated the title uncomfortably and without enthusiasm. Yuigahama responded with a patter of applause.

Turning the page of her paperback, Yukinoshita paused to shoot me a questioning look. "…So where are these coming from?"

"I figured Miss Hiratsuka had something to do with that…" Recently, Miss Hiratsuka had added this advice e-mail thing to the Service Club's list of duties. She said people around the school would send us e-mails with their problems.

Yuigahama peered at the laptop screen to read out the e-mail. "Um, the first message of the day is…from Chiba city, with the username: Master Swordsman General."

Why even bother having a fake name…? It called to mind not only his name but his whole face and figure.

Request for advice from username: Master Swordsman General

I may have M-2 syndrome, but I want to be in love.

Response from the Service Club:
You *can* fall in love, even with M-2 syndrome. Why not muster your courage and try confessing your feelings? Then she's sure to tell you how she feels, too: "I'm sorry."

"......You know he's gonna get rejected?!" After reading it aloud, Yuigahama clued in a little late.

One-sided feelings and heartbreak are just part of being in love, though.

Unfortunately, as you can see, all the requests we'd gotten were garbage. Also, despite how this was supposed to be "Prefecture-Wide," they only ever came from within Chiba city.

Anyway, that was one down, so on to the next. I prompted Yuigahama with a look.

"Right, well, I'll read the next one, then? Um...from username: Woman with stable income (teaching) looking for husband."

Come on, seriously, is there any point in trying to conceal who that is? And it's blatant self-advertising, to boot. She's way too gung ho about this. That username alone tells the whole story.

Request for advice from username: Woman with stable income (teaching) looking for husband
This is embarrassing to admit, but I'm not very good at housekeeping. I'm a bad cook, too, of course. I'm hopelessly anxious about getting married (lol). I don't even know whether I can get married in the first place (lol). I'd like to master cooking at least one dish. Is there anything that men generally like (lol) that's also easy to make and also that men generally like (lol)? Oh, whoops, I wrote that twice (lol). Anyway, is there some kind of easy-to-make meal that will leave a good impression on a man?

"Don't ask your students about this...," I moaned.

Nope. Seriously, actually nope. And all those self-deprecating *lols*? Legitimately, sincerely scary. Nope.

But it seemed the horror of this didn't reach the girls, as the two of them discussed it with no apparent concerns.

"Oh, like beef stew or something? Like the sort of comfort food your mom would make?" suggested Yuigahama.

"A Japanese-style Salisbury steak is a little twist on the standard. I think it might give a unique impression," said Yukinoshita.

Well, both of those suggestions were solid—and that was exactly why they wouldn't work. "Hold on there. That's trying too hard; it comes off as creepy. That'll just bite you in the ass." If a woman makes stuff like that for you, it's easy to assume she's thinking, *Making this is a safe bet (lol)! Men are so easy (lol)!* And I wouldn't like that. I might be a little prejudiced.

"So what would be good, then?" Yukinoshita gave me a piercing glare.

With a rather more nervous look, Yuigahama added, "Oh, I'd really like to know, too...sorta."

"Sounds to me like you guys don't understand what *Mom's cooking* really is. Listen, moms treat sons and daughters completely different. To the boys of the world, Mom's cooking is..." I paused, and Yuigahama leaned forward. *Hmm, it's not like I'm saying anything that amazing, though...*

"...Some random meat fried up with rice on the side. That's Mom's cooking."

"...I shouldn't have bothered asking," Yuigahama muttered.

"I wonder what he's going to say, and then..."

The two of them looked ready to nuke me to Neo Tokyo.

But I had my own point to make. "Anyway, boys have pretty simple tastes. Not to mention, you're cooking every day once you get married, you know?" I said.

Yukinoshita put her hand to her jaw in a thoughtful gesture. "Hmm, that's true. For a daily menu, you need to come up with some go-tos that never get old..."

"Naw, I just mean making anything complicated is a pain in the butt. Easy stuff is best."

"You're taking the househusband approach here?! ...And yet, that's such a realistic way to look at it..." Yuigahama started off surprised, and then a note of resignation crept into her expression.

Yukinoshita breathed a short sigh. "Well, I'll keep that in mind. We can probably include that idea in the reply," she said, and with her usual cool demeanor, she quietly and quickly began typing.

```
Reply from the Service Club:
Beef stew or Japanese-style Salisbury steak are
some ideas, but after taking into account a boy's view
of "Mom's cooking," we would recommend ginger-fried
pork. However, Miss Hiratsuka, shouldn't you priori-
tize your search for a partner?
```

...There really is no point in having usernames.
Someone marry this woman already, seriously.

SS 1

Advice e-mail

from: Woman with stable income (teaching) looking for husband

I don't even know whether I can get married in the first place (lol). I'd like to master cooking at least one dish.

We must wish **them all** the best in their futures.

SA
A

Marriage is life's grave.

Without exception, married people will proudly prattle on about how wonderful it is. How happy they are to say *Honey, I'm home* to someone, or how seeing their kids' sleeping faces enables them to keep working hard the next day…but I'm gonna stop you right there.

If you live with your parents, you'll have someone to say *I'm home* to, and if you want, you can even buy some gargling solution and come home to a hippo. And besides, if all you're seeing of your kids is their sleeping faces, that just means you're living in overtime hell.

Can you really call that happiness?

They're all extolling marriage as true bliss, but the expression in their eyes is just as rotten as mine. They're like zombies luring people into a swamp.

So here I ask you: Can you really call that happiness?

Happiness is like… How should I put it? Like when you see your little sister in the morning when she's humming to herself and making breakfast in the kitchen with an apron on. Maybe I could call it something like that.

Doing just that, I yawned and let my consciousness drift as I waited for my darling little sister to finish making me breakfast.

This is happiness. I'll never need marriage!

Both our parents work, and they'd left the house early that day, as always. They seemed busy. *I really am grateful for their efforts. It's thanks to them that I can live this semblance of a fulfilling lifestyle.*

I do intend to become a househusband eventually, but these days, with the average age of marriage rising and the marriage rate dropping, that might not be so easy. I also hear the divorce rate is rising, too.

Maybe the lifestyle I aspire to is one that's no longer functional, given the current social climate. But wait, would it have worked at *any* point in history? Like the Heian period or something?

Since I might not be able to get married, I would like my parents to continue to work good and hard for a very long time. Sponging off my parents is just the beginning—I'll pull out the wet-vac to suck them entirely dry.

As such ambitions burned in Hachiman Hikigaya's heart, Komachi, opposite me in the kitchen, spun around. It seemed she'd finished making breakfast. She cheerfully brought me my breakfast tray from the kitchen. "Thanks for waiting~."

"Uh-huh."

She put the tray down on the table and took her seat opposite me. The day's menu was toast, salad, omelets…and coffee, I suppose. Pretty American. Or Nagoyan. Looks good, meow.

Komachi first started doing house chores toward the latter half of elementary school, and lately, she's gotten pretty accustomed to it. She's far surpassed me, especially when it comes to cooking, and is already approaching our mom's level.

From our parents' perspective, seeing their child surpass them must be quite moving. I think in the future, I, too, will surpass my father to become an even greater scumbag.

"Sorry you always end up doing this."

"You promised to stop saying that, Bro."

After some trivial sibling conversation, I put my hands together to give my thanks for the blessings of life. It's important to be thankful for your bacon—I learned that from *Silver Spoon*. Also, can't forget to say *Thank you, my twilight* to the bringers of that bacon. It's thanks to Mommy and Daddy working for us that I was able to eat this meal today. Food tastes great when you're not the one working for it. Super-great.

Be that as it may, my eyes unfortunately landed on something less than great.

"I don't like tomatoes," I said, picking up my fork. No matter how great free food is, I'll never be able to see the greatness in those.

But Komachi showed no concern for me. "Yeah, that's why I put them in," she said nonchalantly, without any timidity, and started eating her salad.

...Huh? How does that make sense? Is that not strange?

Did her parents never teach her not to do things that upset people? ...Now that I think about it, no one ever taught me that. As expected of my parents. The ol' laissez-faire method: Just watch and figure it out yourself. What's with this onboarding policy, man? It's like a grouchy old master passing along his techniques to a successor or something.

As her older brother, I had to have a proper talk with her about this now. "Uh...listen...Komachi-chan?"

"You're just so picky, Bro—with people, and food," Komachi replied as she shoveled omelet into her mouth.

Oh, if you're going to be like that, then I have my piece to say, too. I shall tell you the truth of this world... I took my cup of coffee in hand, sipped from it, and puffed out my chest. "That's not really a bad thing. Forcing yourself even when you hate it will just make both parties unhappy."

"Agh...I feel like you're never gonna be able to get married, Bro." Komachi breathed a *good grief* sort of sigh.

What's with that attitude? It's not like I said anything strange. More like I understand that marriage probably isn't gonna happen for me, so could you just not say that out loud? Your big brother tells himself every day that he'll be a househusband to imprint it into his subconscious in his attempt to avoid singledom.

Plus, refusing to bend for the sake of marriage is just part of who I am.

You shouldn't fake who you really are, and people will always have different values, no matter what. If you're raised in different environments, then you're bound to have different preferences, no question. If marriage is failing to recognize those differences and forcibly locking them away for the sake of being together, then that isn't exactly wedded bliss, is it?

My thoughts continued unabated as I ate my omelet. Yeah, it was good.

"There's ketchup."

Well, it's an omelet, so of course there's ketchup. Or what? Were you a mayonnaise type? Are you a mayo maniac? Or a Shino-maniac? That's ultra-relaxing. Komachi wouldn't have any nostalgia about that song, nor would she even know it existed. Thinking about all this, I raised my head to find her face right there in front of me.

She stared at me hard, then leaned forward and gently touched my cheek with her fingertip.

Huh? I thought, but it seemed there had been some ketchup on my cheek. *Then just say so! Your face is too close and it's annoying and embarrassing and kinda like we're newlyweds and it's embarrassing so stop.* I shot her a look in protest.

But Komachi wasn't bothered. She just chuckled. "That was worth a lot of Komachi points."

"If you hadn't added *that*," I said, wolfing down my salad.

She's really not a cute little sister... Though if she weren't always adding comments like that one just now, she'd be supercute. A bitter smile appeared on my lips. Perhaps that smile was why even the tomatoes tasted bitter...

Well, just as I understand Komachi's strengths and flaws, I think she understands me, too. Family is nice and easy.

At the end of the day, it's like—even if you don't get married, just as long as you have a little sister, it's all good, right? Creators, if you're gonna put the main unit or disc into a special edition set, then box the little sister with it. It'll be a real hit.

X   X   X

I went through my usual morning, my typical school day, and then to our regularly scheduled after-school activities. What was unusual that day was the arrival of a slightly different sort of request.

Miss Hiratsuka had come to us with this request and let something land on the desk with a thud.

Yukinoshita's and Yuigahama's faces were side by side as they looked alternately between a magazine and a sheet of paper. Yukinoshita had her eyebrows knit together in consternation, while Yuigahama looked dazed, like she wasn't thinking anything at all.

This seemed to be related to the request, so I popped in from behind to peer down at the desk, wondering what this was about.

The magazine Yuigahama was gaping at was labeled *Chiba* and filled with familiar images and words. It seemed to be one of those publications you'd call a "community magazine." *Huh? Wait, what? Is that thing filled with special info about Chiba? I'd like to subscribe to it; where do I ask?*

Meanwhile, written at the top of the printout Yukinoshita was reading, I could see the word *plan* in bold. Probably some type of proposal.

"Um…Peachy Chiba Weddings," Yuigahama said with a deeply interested *ooh.*

Why's it named like that magical girl show? This was coming off scarily like that song "Dreamin'," so I shifted my eyes over to the part Yuigahama was reading.

The aggressively happy romantic content leaped out at me, and I flinched. Come on, I know for a fact that marriage isn't this ruthlessly positive. "Agh, a marriage special for young people, huh…?" I muttered, annoyed.

But it seemed Miss Hiratsuka's impression of marriage was not so negative. With her pointer finger toward the ceiling, she explained smoothly. "Yes, they're making a community magazine in order to stimulate the local economy. So the local government is working together with bridal shops and hotels with wedding venues and such to make this, with the goal of having the younger generation be more deeply informed about the significance of marriage."

Hmm. So apparently, this community magazine was one of those joint ventures between the government and private industries. Miss Hiratsuka must have brought this magazine as an example.

As Yukinoshita listened to Miss Hiratsuka speak, her eyes traced the lines of words on the proposal sheet. Then she put one hand to her temple, set the paper on the desk, and tapped it. "And what reason might you have for bringing this to us?" Yukinoshita glared at Miss Hiratsuka for a good long moment.

Miss Hiratsuka was at a loss for words. With an *urk*, she averted her eyes in shame. "W-well, um, you know…some higher-ups said our school should help in some fashion, and I ended up in charge, so…" Miss Hiratsuka replied in a faltering manner as Yukinoshita's sharp glare pierced her through.

"Why our school? Why us…?" I complained with a sigh.

Miss Hiratsuka blinked a few times, then suddenly, her gaze turned distant. "You want to know why, huh? Yeah… When orders come down, there is no *why*. That's what it means to have a job."

"I didn't want to hear that. I didn't want to hear about that…" The last vestiges of my will to get a job disappeared all at once… It's funny… when you lose your will to get a job, your desire to get married (= desire to become a dependent) shoots up aggressively… Yeah, well, if everyone starts wanting to become a dependent, it'll do wonders for the marriage rate.

As the battleship of my heart was welcoming the (lifestyle) maintenance crew to its port, Yukinoshita lightly cleared her throat. "The question is, why make us do it?"

"Oh yeah. I mean, this is *your* job, Miss Hiratsuka…" Up till that point, Yuigahama had been engrossed in the community magazine, but when Yukinoshita spoke, she jerked her head up and gave Miss Hiratsuka a curious look.

Miss Hiratsuka hesitated, perhaps flustered under the purity of her gaze. Then she gave a trembling sob. "I—I mean…I don't know what to do about m-marriage…"

Finally, the tears came.

…See what you did? You made her cry.

I looked over at Yuigahama, who looked at Yukinoshita.

"Yukinon…"

Uh, this is your fault, too, Yuigahama…

Seeing Miss Hiratsuka sniffling and sobbing in front of her, plus Yuigahama's tender look, Yukinoshita flinched, then breathed a sigh of resignation. "Agh… We aren't especially knowledgeable about the topic, either, but we'll help."

"...Yeah, thanks." Miss Hiratsuka sniffed and wiped at her tears as she expressed her gratitude to Yukinoshita. The cuteness was unexpected, especially given her age.

Hurry! Hurry up, someone, marry this woman! If not, I'll end up taking her!

× × ×

We poured some tea to calm Miss Hiratsuka, then we began staring at the proposal sheet.

Apparently, the long and short of it was that we'd gotten a page in this community magazine and we were supposed to write some kind of article for it.

"But what should we do?" Yuigahama questioned, folding her arms with a *hmm*.

Indeed, springing this article on us posed a problem. Miss Hiratsuka must have brought this project to us because she'd been struggling with it, too.

Apparently, some pages had already been set aside for this, so it couldn't be canceled now. There were only a few ways we could deal with this.

"We just have to write up something to fill the space, right?" I said. "Okay, so we make the whole page ad space and sell it off. Less work for us, and we make money, too. It's perfect."

"Hikigaya...you can't do that." Miss Hiratsuka shook her head, her expression weary.

That's a no-go, huh...? I'd thought it was a pretty good idea, though. Agency style: You sell the space elsewhere and make a profit.

"The issue is the deadline... How much time do we have?" Yukinoshita put her cup down with a *clink* and checked the calendar.

Miss Hiratsuka followed her gaze. "Submission is next week, and it'll take another week to finish proofreading, I suppose."

"That's not much time." Yukinoshita shot her an accusing look.

But Miss Hiratsuka just smiled wryly, looking tired. "When you have a job, you'll find yourself pushing work to the back burner without even thinking about it…and that goes double if it's something you don't want to start."

"Oh, I kinda get that." Yeah. Yeah, I really do. The more you don't want to do it, the more you keep putting it off. That's why it's easier, mentally speaking, to just dash something off if you really hate it. The world is overflowing with frightening rush jobs of that nature, and yet, some of the people responsible for it still get paid, which is the truly terrifying thing. I don't wanna end up like that, so I figure it's best for me to not get a job after all.

But it wasn't like we were getting paid for this, and I doubted it would have to be quality. "So let's just write up some bullshit and put it in," I said.

Yukinoshita shook her head. "A text-only section would be tough, too."

"So you mean we should use layout and design to make it look legit?"

With the power of layout and design, you can take plain text and slap something together. You know, like how they often do with anime—those shows that fill up space with cool lettering or narration. It always makes you suspect they just failed to finish the animation frames on schedule, but with some real stylish textual production, the audience will interpret it in a rather more positive way.

"That would work, if we had the time, but it would be difficult. Besides, do you think an amateur's design could fill the space properly?"

"Aren't there templates out there of old work? We can just combine a bunch of them and dump in the text," I said, and just for an instant, Yukinoshita considered it with a *hmm*.

Meanwhile, Yuigahama was getting left behind in this conversation. She tugged on Miss Hiratsuka's sleeve with an expression of terror. "M-Miss Hiratsuka, they're kinda scaring me…"

"It sounds to me like they can get things done. But still, it's not exactly what you expect of high school students…"

Yukinoshita ignored Miss Hiratsuka's wry smile. She must have reached a conclusion, as she put her hand to her temple in exasperation and sighed. "Agh, slacking off is the one thing you're smart about…"

"I just value efficiency."

"Regardless, no. The request is for an article that feels like it was created by high schoolers."

Well, that was a reasonable point. If they'd wanted something professional, they wouldn't have passed the baton to us in the first place.

Something high school students would create... What do all those honchos in town hall think is high schooler–ish? Is it the energy of a high school basketball player? Or, like, the chattery glee of a modern high school girl?

I reflected on myself, then examined Yukinoshita once more. "Then this whole project is a nonstarter, since neither of us is exactly a typical high schooler," I said.

"...Indeed." Yukinoshita's shoulders drooped, as if I'd more or less convinced her, and she looked away.

"Normally, you decide on what you're going to do first. If you're thinking about filling space first and foremost... You kids are so jaded," Miss Hiratsuka said with exasperation, or perhaps a bit of wonder, after she watched our conversation.

We were well aware of that, too. I sighed.

No, wait.

There was someone...some normal high school student... When the idea hit me suddenly, my eyes turned in that direction. "Yuigahama, you're ordinary. This is your big moment."

"You don't have to put it like that!" Yuigahama was huffily indignant.

But Yukinoshita followed up, her face serious. "Could we ask this of you, Yuigahama?"

"I don't really know what to think when you ask *now*, of all times!" Despite receiving a long-awaited opportunity to do her thing, Yuigahama complained, tearing up.

I think her normalness is pretty valuable. Personally, I believe it helps Yukinoshita in a lot of ways. It's okay for her to be normal.

Yuigahama moaned in reluctance, but when Yukinoshita gave her a wordless glance, she moaned some more, then seemed to make up her mind.

Yuigahama folded her arms.

Then she put her head in her hands.

Then she stared vacantly into the air.

It seemed she'd used her head too much and had caused herself brain trauma. She had a dazed look on her face, as if she'd thought her soul right out of her body.

But then suddenly, she clapped her hands. "Oh, we could get people to send in designs for a wedding dress or something!"

"I doubt too many people can draw up designs like that," I countered. I'd considered something like that, too, but it would be a difficult plan to execute. It would also be difficult to find that many people to do designs. It wasn't the time to be going around to each and every person, asking, *Will you wind? Yes/no.*

Yuigahama pressed her hands against her head as hard as she could, then jolted forward. "Um, then…a wedding dress contest! Or something?"

"Timewise, it would be difficult for us to take applications from the whole school," Yukinoshita answered.

Since the deadline to hand it in was next week, ensuring the whole school was notified while simultaneously organizing the event would be impossible. Even if we were to shrink the editing time and sync up the schedule accordingly, an extra week wouldn't change much.

I felt bad, since Yuigahama was trying to come up with things for us, but you can't win when you're fighting against the man. Well, this wasn't really the man. Just a deadline. They should get rid of deadlines altogether.

Yuigahama tried again, racking her brains with an audible *mrrrr-rrg*, but then she seemed to give up. Her arms unfolded. "Um, marriage, marriage, marriage… Hmm, I don't really know. It just doesn't feel real to me, I guess."

"Well," I said, "it's not something we think about much, at our age." Next year, I'd basically be old enough to get married legally, but it didn't really feel immediate to me. The two girls had to feel the same.

But then I heard a very serious-sounding mutter. "I guess so… When I was your age, I wasn't thinking about it at all…"

Yuigahama and I automatically went silent, looking away without a word.

"…"

"…"

Uh, so what do we do about the dour mood in here? This isn't the time to be gazing out the window, Miss Hiratsuka.

Meanwhile, Yukinoshita alone seemed to fall silent for slightly different reasons. She put her hand to her chin thoughtfully. "Thinking about it…," she muttered.

"Hmm?" I responded.

Yukinoshita nodded twice as if she had convinced herself of something. "We aren't thinking about it, and that may mean an opinion poll would make a good topic."

"Ohhh, I see! It might be kinda fun to have everyone fill out some kind of survey." Yuigahama applauded.

An opinion poll or survey, huh? It did seem like a convenient plan for filling up the space. For graduation albums and stuff, they have those *Top Three People Most Likely to X.* When you're doing those, could you not force in the really stupid, pointless category—*People Most Likely to Become Company Presidents in the Future*—out of consideration for people whose names aren't listed elsewhere? The kindness just makes it hurt more. Oh yeah, that reminds me that the last page of my graduation album is completely blank. Was that a misprint or something?

Maybe they should just make this community magazine thing blank and add some title like *To the Future-To Love Marriage-* and make it a page for collecting signatures. Then just slap on something that fits, like *You fill these pages.* That'd fool some people.

I was giving it due consideration in my own way, but Yukinoshita seemed to be seriously pondering the matter, too. "Surveying the whole school or grade level would be too time-consuming, so it may be best to narrow it down to one class…"

"That doesn't seem statistically useful." Just one class is actually grad album level—far from valid statistical parameters for an opinion poll. Not like we were doing an academic survey, though, so it didn't really matter.

Of course, Yukinoshita was aware of this. "There's no way around it, in this situation. If we come up with a good page layout and put in an editorial write-up and such, it should look fairly decent."

Then Miss Hiratsuka, who had been watching us until this point, said, "Hmm, a write-up, huh? That'll be your job, then, Hikigaya."

"Why me...?" *There are two other people here...* I had a hunch that essay-wise, Yuigahama is pretty...*y'know*, and Yukinoshita's content would be kinda...*y'know*, but I can confidently say I'm not much better, y'know! And hey, wasn't this originally the teacher's job?

I'd poured almost my whole heart into that *Why me*. Miss Hiratsuka heard my plea, then told me her very clear-cut reason: "You always write such asinine reports and essays. This'll be a snap for you."

Nobody would do it after hearing that... Come on, where's your leadership skills?

I must really have looked reluctant, as Miss Hiratsuka combed back her hair with a hand and winked at me. "Content aside, I do think highly of your writing ability."

When she smiled at me like that, it got harder to resist. "...Well, it's not like I couldn't write it..."

Embarrassed, I looked away. My eyes landed on Yukinoshita, who was pressing her temple for some reason. "It seems this is gonna be a tough editing project for me..."

Uh, I didn't ask you, though... Actually, I feel like you'd red pen the whole thing, so please no. Let's make our editorial policy to water the Hachi-plant with compliments!

Seeing Yukinoshita's sigh, Miss Hiratsuka smirked mischievously. "Oh, so you'll keep an eye on him for me, Yukinoshita? Then I can rest easy."

"...I don't mind doing that much, at least." Yukinoshita jerked her head away grumpily and adjusted her collar.

Uh, but I didn't ask you, though... Come on, are you chief editor now?

"All righty, then! Now we just have to think up survey questions," Yuigahama said, sitting back down in her chair. Anyway, since we'd come up with an objective, we'd have to get cracking.

Miss Hiratsuka turned to face us once more. "Well then, before we pass the survey on to everyone, why don't we do a little trial run?"

We rummaged around the room to scrounge up some paper, and then we all came up with some questions that seemed appropriate. Yukinoshita compiled them into a list, Miss Hiratsuka left for a bit to make copies, and then we all wrote down our own answers. Once we were about done, Miss Hiratsuka scanned the room.

"Okay, let's see what we've got," she said, then took up one of the sheets she'd collected from us.

Q. What income level do you seek in a partner?
A. Over 1,000,000 yen

"Hikigaya..."

"Hikki..."

Yukinoshita and Yuigahama both said my name with dismay, looking at me with dull eyes.

"Hold on there. How'd you know that was me?"

"You can tell just by looking at your writing..." Yuigahama glared at me.

Yukinoshita brushed her hair off her shoulder. "Do you believe you're worth that much? You have no friends, you're abysmal in sciences, your employment prospects are doubtful, and you have no future. And you have the eyes of a dead fish..."

"Shut up. There are tons of soft souls out there in the world who'll give similar answers."

You see it a lot on those marriage-hunting specials they do on the variety segments on the evening news—women in their thirties who come for those marriage-hunting parties will write answers like this. But the people who meet their standards are in real high demand, so they won't go to those parties in the first place. I wouldn't say these women are dreaming too much—it's more accurate to say they're not looking at reality clearly enough.

"W-well, um, you know. It's good to set your sights high, uh-huh."

For once, Miss Hiratsuka was on my side. *Thank you, Teacher! So… what was written on that paper hidden behind your back?*

"A-anyway! We've got our questions, so let's start sampling!" Miss Hiratsuka must have noticed my rotten look, as she bounded to her feet.

X   X   X

Yuigahama volunteered to go do the sampling, so in the meantime, I zoned out and waited for her. Miss Hiratsuka reviewed her own answers to the survey, muttering something as she reexamined herself.

As for Yukinoshita, she was reading her usual paperback. Her shoulders suddenly twitched, and she closed her book.

The door banged open.

"There were still some people around, so I got them to fill out the surveys!" Yuigahama marched in proudly, holding up a stack of papers. *Hey, is this Yukinoshita's special superpower? It's like my family cat when Komachi comes home…*

"Thank you, Yuigahama. Sorry for making you do that," Yukinoshita said to her.

Yuigahama sat down in her usual spot and replied, "No, it's totally okay. It looked like the only people still around were from our class anyway."

As Yuigahama said, of the papers she spread out for us, only a few had been filled in. However, Yuigahama was probably the only one of us who would have been able to get this much done.

"Well, if I asked people to do it, they wouldn't give us anything," I said.

"Indeed," replied Yukinoshita. "If you were to attempt that, Hikigaya, I'm sure you'd sound like you were selling religion or some dubious product."

"You got it. They just couldn't handle my bad boy charisma." Her remark had stung a little, so I snapped back at her. Yukinoshita breathed an exasperated sigh.

Another sigh followed before she was even done. "In your case, the scary part is that I think you really would start a religion…," Miss Hiratsuka said with a perfectly straight face.

Come on, it's like you actually mean it...

But anyway, if Yukinoshita had been the one to go try to get these filled out, I think it would have made them wary. They'd gently reject her attempt, and that would be the end of that.

Even I was on the verge of sighing, but Yuigahama intervened. "Come on, guys. How about we just look at these?"

As prompted, we fanned out the papers on the desk and inspected them. Yuigahama read out one.

Q. What do you think is a good job for a marriage partner?
A. I want to marry a voice actor!

I immediately understood who was responsible for that.

"Okay, okay, next. Wait, he's not even in our class..."

Instantly flicking aside Zaimokuza's paper, I looked at each of the sheets in turn.

Q. Do you have any anxieties about marriage?

A. No way am I cooking. Or cleaning. Not happening.

A. Relationship with my mother-in-law, whether I'd be living with the in-laws, inheritance and such. Since I have a lot of siblings.

A. I'm anxious about where Hayama/Hachiman is going.

Huh, I thought, looking at the answers and feeling slightly weary. Especially that last one. They didn't have to write their names—it was obvious who'd written each one. I could finish this game without looking at the walk-through.

"I can basically tell who wrote these..."

"Well, they are from our class."

Indeed, as Yuigahama said, all these responses had clearly come from our classmates. Probably Miura, Kawa-something, and Ebina…

You know, Miura is very consistent in her own way. I can respect that. As expected of the queen.

Kawa-something… Sounds like nothing goes her way. It's very Sachi Usuko, so I do sincerely hope she does her best to find happiness.

And Ebina's…you know.

"I dunno if we should print this." Yukinoshita tilted her head, considering.

Uh, that's not even worth thinking about. You know it's no good…

It seemed I was not the only one thinking this. Flipping through the stack of papers, Miss Hiratsuka mused, "Hmm. These answers seem a little divorced from reality."

"Are you in any position to be saying that…?" I gave Miss Hiratsuka a hard look.

Yuigahama, meanwhile, ignored me, folding her arms as she pondered the matter. "But we wouldn't know the good and bad stuff about being married, so there's no way for us to answer. I bet there's plenty you wouldn't know unless you've experienced it yourself…"

Well, my own personal sample is just my parents, and it's not like I observe them consciously. Maybe I'd find another answer if I thought more closely, but it seems incredibly difficult to put yourself in someone else's shoes and try to think from their perspective. This is especially true at puberty, when you're at your most self-conscious.

No matter what you do, you can't become anyone else.

And if you feel that way even with your parents, actually getting married and living together with a stranger is bound to be far more difficult than you can imagine.

As I pondered, Yukinoshita opened her mouth as if she'd just remembered something. "I may have an idea, if we need a young person who's experienced something similar already."

"Huh? Really?" Yuigahama asked with deep interest, and Yukinoshita smiled wide.

"Yes, when it comes to understanding the trials of taking care of a deadbeat in your life, then perhaps she knows best of all."

Yukinoshita's response was very specific, and I couldn't help getting sparkly eyes.

Huh? You know someone like that? For real? Sounds like the type that might support me. Hurry up and introduce me to her, please. Now I've basically won at life.

…Or so I thought.

$$\times \quad \times \quad \times$$

Not even an hour later, the idea Yukinoshita had spoken of walked into the clubroom. This was indeed a familiar face. Truly, I hadn't seen it since this morning.

"So why Komachi?" My eyes, which had earlier been sparkling, took a turn to stinking rotten. Meanwhile, Komachi was wearing a beaming smile as she stood in front of the door.

"Did I not say? She understands the trials of caring for a deadbeat."

That deadbeat is absolutely, without a doubt me, isn't it…? Well, she hasn't said I should be dead, so the insult is relatively mild. Maybe she's in a good mood today?

Once Yukinoshita had summarized the situation, Komachi nodded. "I see, I see. Please show me that survey." She stuck out her hand, and Yukinoshita handed over the stack of paper. Komachi looked at every page, nodding. "…I see! I feel like I've got a sense of the trends you're all concerned with."

My sister is known for her skill in picking up ideas quickly and dealing with issues as they come, and this was no exception. Well, Zaimokuza aside, Miura's and Kawasaki's anxieties about future marriage were understandable. Ebina's was not even worth discussing; Komachi and the rest of us seemed to reach the same conclusion on that one.

"Yeah, so we were just wondering about what we should do next," said Yuigahama.

"We can't simply submit this as is… If you have any ideas, we would be grateful for your help," Yukinoshita added.

Komachi rubbed her temple with a finger as she considered. "Hmm, hmm… Ah! Komachi's got an idea!" And then she clapped her hands.

I'm suspicious of these strangely dramatic gestures… It really looks like she's cooking up another of her nefarious schemes…

But the others took no notice of my anxieties, looking at her with hope in their eyes. As the center of attention, Komachi raised her pointer finger and proudly declared, "What I see from this opinion poll now is that all these people have staggeringly low levels of brideness."

"What's *brideness*…?" I said.

"Don't sweat the details. Basically, we address the question of how to become more bride-like instead!" Komachi chirped. Not only did she casually ignore my question, she'd even started to twist this plan in the direction she wanted it to go.

Miss Hiratsuka said, "Hmm, sort of like a bride-training special?"

"Komachi likes that phrase! I'll take it! ☆" Komachi did this funny gesture like she was making a note on her palm, stood from her seat, and declared loudly, "Now then…the bride training starts immediately! The heart-fluttering brideness showdown~! ♪ Duh-duh-duh-duuuh!"

Yukinoshita, Miss Hiratsuka, and I all looked at Komachi doubtfully, but Yuigahama applauded with inexplicable enthusiasm.

"Again, what even is *brideness*…?"

My question would go eternally unanswered.

✕ ✕ ✕

Komachi had some stuff to set up for this brideness showdown, apparently, so it was decided we would hold it later.

And then it was the day of the event. We all gathered in the clubroom, but then the girls disappeared off somewhere at Komachi's behest. I waited a while for them to call for me.

In the meantime, I was left alone in the Service Club room, forced to kill time. Not that I minded. I've always been good at holding down the fort.

While I was absorbed in the paperback I had on me, my cell phone buzzed. I checked it to see Komachi had sent me a text.

…'Come to the home ec room'? Just what is she gonna make us do?

Still, I generally meet my sister's demands. That's just who I am.

I ditched the clubroom and headed to the home ec room.

The empty hallways after school are so nice. They're so silent you might forget about their usual clamor. However, as I got closer to the home ec room, it became strangely noisy. I could occasionally even hear something like yelling.

Come on… Now I'm scared of going in there…

But I'd already reached the door. Rallying my courage, I opened it.

And there I saw Komachi waiting for me in an apron. "Oh, you're finally here. All right, Bro, let's get started."

"Start? Start what?" I asked.

Komachi boldly posed with her hands on her hips. "Bride training! It starts right now! The heart-fluttering ☆ brideness showdown~ ♪," she cried, and then she smoothly pulled a ladle out from behind her. *Hammerspace? Really?*

Komachi held up the ladle like a microphone and turned around. "Showdown number one is cooking!"

Behind her were Yukinoshita, Yuigahama, and Miss Hiratsuka, all in aprons just like Komachi. Farther behind them was a set of table and chairs, and two familiar faces were sitting there.

"Please and thank you to all our judges!" Komachi called, and one of the two in back waved.

"I have no idea why you called me here, but…good luck, everyone!"

"Herm, story premises these days are indeed so deep they require explanation… So be it! This Master Swordsman General shall resign himself to this fate!"

It was Totsuka and Zaimokuza. Had Komachi invited them here?

I stood there, confused, and Komachi indicated a seat at that table. "Go on, Bro. Take a seat at the judges' table."

So apparently, the ones in aprons were going to cook, and it was the job of those at the table to be judges. I had some misgivings about this, but if I were to show reluctance, I knew she would do whatever it took to force me into it.

I obediently sat down in the chair she'd set out for me.

There were, frankly, many things about this turn of events that I could complain about, but I would just go for the one at the top of the list. "Should Totsuka be sitting with us? Hey, is he in the right place?" I asked Komachi in a whisper, just to be sure, but my sister casually ignored me and turned back to the other girls. *The cold shoulder, huh? Harsh.*

"The theme here is Mom's cooking, specifically what boys want. First up to bat is Yui!" Komachi called out to her, and Yuigahama boldly stepped up front. In her hands was a plate topped with the kind of silver cover you see in fancy restaurants.

"Um, you're serving...?" Komachi asked.

"Japanese-style Salisbury steak!" Yuigahama answered as she popped off the silver cover and boldly unveiled her masterpiece.

But when Komachi saw it, her reaction was not favorable.

"...Whaaa?" Komachi violently cringed away.

No surprise there. That blackened substance and goopy sauce. The grated daikon was dyed deep brown; the onions, devastated.

...Japanese-style? What about this is Japanese-style? It looks more like a barren volcano, and there's no style of any sort to be had... If you told me that was Mount Kilauea, I think I'd believe it. And which part of that is even hamburger? Is it even edible, actually?

Zaimokuza, however, ignored my cringing. He must have been excited about eating a girl's homemade cooking, as he gallantly reached out his hand. "Grfem, grfem. Oh, no, no, no! Yoshi-*no* Nanjou! There is an old saying: You cannot judge a book by its cover. I warrant the form of these rations conceals its brilliance..." Zaimokuza made like he was saying something cool for once, but his declaration was not only actually completely false, it accomplished nothing.

He spooned some of the Salisbury steak into his mouth, and then, as if the shock of divine revelation were running through him, his eyes flared wide. "Nghhh!" he moaned. "Bleagh." He gave a very plain, quiet groan, then fell face-first onto the desk, following which he did not even twitch. Utter silence fell.

And the culprit was in this very room...

Komachi gave Zaimokuza a long, hard look, and once she had confirmed resuscitation was unlikely, she spun around to face me. "Uhhh, Snowflake's out, so next...Bro."

"Huh?" I pointed at myself, confused, and Yuigahama's cooking was slid in front of me.

"Ngh…" I engaged in a staring contest with this brutal image, then fell silent.

Though Zaimokuza did have a reputation for obnoxious overreactions, seeing someone get hit that hard will drain your confidence. I sat frozen there as Yuigahama fiddled with the bun in her hair and gave a little *ah-ha-ha* to cover her embarrassment.

"Y-you don't have to f-force yourself to eat it, Hikki…" She looked away, eyes listing downward, laughing an empty laugh.

Oh, I don't want to force myself, either. I don't like having anything forced down my throat, after all. Reason should always come before force.

But I couldn't call surrender here, either. I should be thankful for the blessings of life, and Zaimokuza had already sacrificed himself, and… Well. Anyway. Might as well, y'know.

Oh, and most importantly, I couldn't make Totsuka eat this.

In an attempt to find my courage, I looked over at Totsuka beside me.

"Hachiman? What's wrong?" My sudden look must have confused him, as he tilted his head, smiling brightly.

I want to protect this smile…

Right now, I am the only one who can. No more reason. It's time for force.

With determination, I took up my chopsticks, grabbed the plate, and sloshed it into my mouth all at once.

Every crunch and munch and slurp was a whole season's worth of *Battlefield Baseball* in flavor.

"Hikki…" I got the feeling that Yuigahama's eyes were a little moist as she looked at me, but frankly, my own eyes were so moist I really couldn't say.

As everyone watched and held their breath, I managed to swallow it down.

The home ec room was filled with silence, the only sound the *clink* of me putting my chopsticks down.

I breathed a short sigh and slowly said, "Um...well, let's put it this way. If you brace yourself and force it down, it could be edible..."

Forget brideness, I'm having doubts about her humanness.

"How is that comment supposed to make me feel?!" Yuigahama cried out, a little heartbroken.

If you're gonna be like that, then put in a little more effort... I sure as heck did.

"When you say that looking so green in the face..." Yukinoshita was looking exasperated and going "Good grief" as Komachi smoothly lined up beside her.

"Next is Yukino!" she prompted.

So Yukinoshita carried over her own dish. Just like Yuigahama's a moment ago, this platter was also covered with one of those silver lids you pop off.

"Announce your creation, please!"

"Paella..." Yukinoshita revealed the dish to show a pretty paella.

Yuigahama peered at the plate and cried out in admiration. "Ohhh~, Italian food!"

"Paella comes from Spain," Yukinoshita said flatly.

Yuigahama was confused. "Huh? But they have it at Italian restaurants... Huh?"

I understood the feeling. It's true they have paella at Saize. They write *(paella)* next to the Mediterranean-style pilaf.

This was the paella carried before us judges. The seafood dish was loaded with meat and vegetables, and the saffron fried rice looked brilliant, too. I could almost feel the wind of the distant Mediterranean... Not like I've ever been to the Mediterranean, though.

Since I'd finished off Yuigahama's meal just a moment ago, I decided to let Totsuka go first this time. Yukinoshita had made this, so there was no need for concern.

"Go ahead," I said, yielding it to him.

Totsuka beamed a smile, immediately taking his spoon in hand. Then he took a bite. "Wow, you really are a great cook, Yukinoshita!"

"It's nothing much. It's just a question of practice." This wasn't

Yukinoshita being modest—she believed it sincerely and spoke with her usual calm.

Following Totsuka, I decided to have some, too. There was absolutely nothing to nitpick here: The rice was properly cooked, the ingredients were balanced, and the presentation was appetizing. But it didn't come off all that wifely...

"It's as good as you'd expect, so I can't really comment..." As I was thinking that I didn't particularly have anything to say, Yuigahama raised her hand.

"Me too! I want some, too!"

"Okeydoke, let's all have some afterward, okay~?" Komachi cut in, gently pushing Yuigahama aside. "Well then, next is Komachi's. Here we go, beef stew!"

Komachi brought this out without any particular airs, but I knew better than any of them just what a good cook Komachi was. It was good, as always. But, like, why was she even participating? I've got no intention of giving her away, so there's no point in her cultivating brideness.

"Yeah, well, you know, it's the usual," I said. "Also, that's a manipulative choice."

"Ngh, our closeness backfires...," Komachi said with a click of her tongue.

Totsuka quickly slid in with a supportive comment. "But it's really good, though?" His warm words were artless and straightforward, which gave them such an edge of truth it brought Komachi to tears.

Sob. "You're a good person, Totsuka... You have a high brideness stat..."

"I think so, too...," I agreed. Frankly, Totsuka has far and away the most. Komachi and I both sighed for different reasons.

But Komachi shook her head and snapped herself out of it. "Ah, wake up, Komachi! Now it's time for our star, Miss Hiratsuka."

Appropriate for such a title, Miss Hiratsuka put on a bold smile brimming with confidence and strode up front.

"What did you make, Miss Hiratsuka?" I asked.

"Heh-heh-heh. This!" She lifted the silver lid with a "Ta-daa!" to reveal a brown meaty plate. It was a huge serving of meat and bean sprouts, with a big bowl of rice on the side.

It was meat, meat, meat, ready to whet the instincts and awaken the wild beast within. The fragrant scent stimulated the appetite in such a way that my stomach went from full to empty.

This combo was a familiar one. There was no mistaking it.

"Th-this is…just meat with bean sprouts, fried up with *yakiniku* sauce poured on it!" I cried.

"Does this count as cooking…?" Yukinoshita seemed a little confused.

But Miss Hiratsuka ignored her and asked me, full of confidence, "What do you think, Hikigaya?"

This is so frustrating! But I'm feeling it! (The flavor.)

Regrettable as it is, I'm forced to acknowledge it… "It's good… It's so good… This *yaki* sauce is great…"

"Compliment *me*." Miss Hiratsuka glared at me, a vein popping in her forehead.

Uh, but if that counts as cooking, then I can do that myself… Menu-wise, that's pretty low brideness, you know?

X   X   X

In the end, cooking alone wasn't enough to measure brideness, so the contest moved on to the next stage.

"All right, next is the bride quiz: What would you do?!" Komachi announced. "Come on, come on, sit, sit." With barely an explanation, she beckoned the girls over to a long table and made them sit in a row. Meanwhile, Totsuka was still left in a judge's seat, and Zaimokuza's corpse was abandoned on the spot. As a member of the Service Club, I was unable to deny Komachi's request for help and had no choice but to obediently do what she told me.

"Now I'm going to pose brideness evaluation questions to all of you. Everyone, please put yourself in the position of a wife as you write your answers."

Hmm, meaning we're going to do some case studies in quiz format? So those seats at the long table are for the people answering. Uh-huh. Then it was obvious where I should be sitting.

"Right then, let's get to it... Wait, why are you sitting there, Bro?"

"'Cause I aspire to be a househusband."

Komachi questioned my seating choice, but my answer was extremely simple. Earlier, I'd been working as judge, so I hadn't been able to participate in the cooking showdown—but I've got way more brideness than these people. *Now, I will show you what it means to be a bride.*

"You can do it, Hachiman!" Totsuka waved at me from the judges' seats, and I replied with a grin.

Komachi gave us the smile of one who has given up. "Oh well. Then let's get started-. Question: 'Your mother-in-law has complained about how you clean. What do you do now?' Please write your answers on your boards!"

Oh, we have boards? Indeed, a mini–white board was in front of me, with a dry-erase pen. *When did Komachi set this up...?*

Without hesitation, I swiftly wrote my response. Since I had some time after finishing, I glanced around at the others to see Yuigahama groaning and Yukinoshita's pen flowing across the board, though her face was stony. Miss Hiratsuka muttered to herself as she scribbled aggressively.

Once she saw we were all done, Komachi called, "Right, then! Answers! Bam!" She pointed at us in order, right to left, and one after another we revealed our boards.

First was Yuigahama. With a cry of "Here we go!" She lifted up her board dramatically.

"'Say I'm sorry and do it over.'"

It was a Yuigahama-like answer. But I've seen on TV that if you don't get along with your mother-in-law, then no matter how you apologize, you'll get beaten down hard, so I can't say that's a good rule of thumb... Sounds like a rough situation...

Next, Yukinoshita revealed her answer, looking disinterested.

"'Explain how my way of cleaning is more logical in every way.'"

Ohhh, this feels like The Yukinoshita Way, all right. She'd argue her mother-in-law down, so no problems there. But the price you pay is that everyone else fights, too. I mean, the husband would be losing arguments, I'm sure, making it a rough situation for everyone else.

Then Miss Hiratsuka chuckled with confidence and answered:

"'Speak with my fists.'"

Hmm. Conversing with physical language. That's really, huh, like someone who's watched too much *shonen* anime and thinks everything can be solved by a one-on-one fight. Under the most optimistic interpretation possible, you could say this allows for some opposition while you strive for reconciliation. Under the interpretation of a normal person, it's like, *What the hell is she talking about?*

Finally, it was my turn.

I flipped up my board.

"'I'd make her miso soup stronger.'"

Ensuring your revenge releases stress, and plus, if you can distract from the initial problem by introducing a new cause for conflict, then she won't complain about the cleaning anymore. It's kind of like getting even for what happened in Edo while you're in Nagasaki. And to top it all off, if you can chip away at her health with unhealthy levels of sodium, then you've basically won...

"Oh-ho-. That's a unique answer... Well, that's a no for both the teacher and my brother." Sweeping her gaze over the answers, Komachi made an X with her fingers and a wry smile with her lips.

No good, huh? Well, I guess weakening her health with too much salt is rather unrealistic. It's better to go for sugar instead, then? I feel like sweetness is less likely to get noticed than saltiness.

Man, none of these quiz answers are any good, huh...? I was thinking to myself when Komachi slipped a board out from behind her back. It seemed she did have a model answer.

"The model answer, in Komachi terms, is this: 'Complain to your mother about it and try again tomorrow.'"

"That's a weirdly realistic answer!" Yuigahama said with a slight cringe.

It's true. You can really tell that she's just trying so hard, even as she suffers. Uh, so is some relative of ours giving her trouble?

Considering what a heavy answer she'd just come up with, Komachi didn't seem too bothered. She cheerfully and calmly moved on. "Onward and upward-. Our next question is this," she said, and suddenly her tone turned theatrical. "'Tomorrow is Christmas. But the hubby's a useless good-for-nothing, so this month might be tight…'" Komachi sniffled and put on a sad look.

Yukinoshita muttered, "Oh my, just like a certain someone."

"Right?" Yuigahama gave a big nod.

"Well, some men are like that. Supporting them is what good wives do," Miss Hiratsuka gravely replied.

Hey? Guys, could you please not say things like that while looking at me?

All three of them were talking, causing Komachi to pause in her reading of the question. She put her hand on her waist and drew her eyebrows together. "We're still in the middle of the question-… 'So in this situation, what do you do about presents for the kids?'" After reading it to the end this time, Komachi tilted her head cutely. Taking that as our signal, we all started writing out answers.

The ticktock of the second hand on the clock was joined by the squeak of the dry-erase markers. When she figured enough time had passed, Komachi called out, "Time's up! Right then, answers! Bam!"

Just like last time, she started with Yuigahama.

"'Cheap toys.'"

Taking it down a level, huh? Well, that was the safest option. But kids know way more about what toys are worth than adults do, so I think they'd kinda notice the difference… But maybe that would result in socially perceptive kids.

Yukinoshita was next.

"'Books.'"

I see. It depends on the book you give them, but the wonderful experience of reading could well be an invaluable source of happiness. Good performance for the cost. Very much the sort of opinion you'd get from a bookworm.

Next was the beaming Miss Hiratsuka.

"'Blu-ray box set of a great anime.'"

That's just what you *want.*

Well, last was me.

"'Explain that Santa doesn't give presents to bad children.'"

...Which was something my father told me. That bastard... What a thing to say to me when I was still a child... My mother did get me a proper present after that, so it was okay, but I had already made up my young mind to go take down Santa...

Seeing all the answers, Komachi smacked herself on the forehead. "Awww, it looks like none of you actually listened to the question. The point of this one is how you deal with the problem," she said, wagging her finger. It seemed the question had not been asking what you give them. "And so, the Komachi answer is this." She pulled out her board to show us and read it out.

"'Let your parents handle it.'"

"Really...?" In her exasperation, Yukinoshita gave Komachi a chilly look.

Komachi waggled her finger with a *tsk, tsk, tsk*. "It's okay. Grandma and Grandpa will be super-duper sweet on the grandkids. Source: Komachi."

Seeing Komachi point to herself, I suddenly remembered. Now that she mentioned it, she was right. Back when I was still a tiny grand-kid, Grandma and Grandpa had been real nice. "Well, that's true," I said. "But once there's a younger kid, the attention shifts."

"The melancholy of the eldest child." Miss Hiratsuka cracked a teasing smile.

Aw, I wouldn't even call it melancholy. Right now, I'm probably the one in our house sweetest on Komachi anyway.

The girl in question looked over at the judges' seats. "Um, so having seen all this, Judge Totsuka, what are your thoughts in Totsuka terms?" she asked.

Totsuka had been observing all this time. He mulled over the question, complete with thinking noises, then grinned. "Getting books as a present is really nice, isn't it?"

Okay, now I know what I'm getting him for Christmas this year.

It'll be a book. But what kind of book...? He's in the tennis club, after all, so maybe a tennis-y one? Or some kind of classic fairy tale, novel, or story. My recommendation there is *The Little Prince*. Okay, then I'll cover both bases and go with *The Prince of Tennis*!

As I was pondering this, Totsuka's interview time came to an end, and Komachi took over again as MC. "Okeydoke! Thank you very much! Righty then, this is your last question-." With that, her dramatic flair returned for the next question. "'Lately, the hubby's been coming home late... He couldn't be...cheating? What do you do?' Okay, answers on your boards!"

In the answer seats, Yuigahama was groaning to herself in thought; Yukinoshita was silent, her face a mask except for the occasional smirk; while Miss Hiratsuka was muttering something as she clenched her fists and enthusiastically cracked her knuckles.

Maybe it's late to be saying this, but I don't like being in this seat...

Hoping to make this end sooner, I quickly scribbled my answer on my board, and then Komachi told us time was up. "And time-. All right, answers all at once, please." Komachi flung her hands in front of her, and this time, we all revealed our responses simultaneously.

"'Worry.'" Yuigahama's response was already worrying.

"'Give him the third degree.'" Yukinoshita's tone was sharp as a blade.

"'Sanctions administered with a fist,'" Miss Hiratsuka said while clenching a fist of her own.

"'Get a divorce and wring a settlement and child support out of it,'" I said as I put out my sign.

Komachi examined each answer, nodded, and *hmm*'d. "That's everyone, huh?"

Following Komachi's eyes as she examined each answer with care, I scanned the other answers, too. My eyes stopped on one. "Give him the third degree? What? Scary..."

Yukinoshita tilted her head, her expression blank. "Oh, perhaps I meant 'interrogate him.' But that's about the same thing, isn't it?" She smiled sweetly.

Yikes. What the hell? I wasn't the only one freaked out—Totsuka and Yuigahama were, too, of course, and even Miss Hiratsuka was a little taken aback.

But it seemed it was not an unacceptable answer, in Komachi terms. "Aside from my brother's, these answers are generally on the right track. But Komachi's idea of a correct answer is this." She held up her own board. "'Believe in him.'" This one is worth a lot of Komachi points."

Komachi's solution did make for a nice story, and all the girls gave little *ohhh*s of admiration. Her understanding was rather deep for a middle schooler—or maybe she had that tendency to dream because she was a middle schooler? No matter how you slice it, though, if you pick this answer and they *are* cheating, you'll be in for a world of pain.

I don't think trust is a good thing, necessarily, at least not in all situations. Mistrust—suspicion, in other words—will defend you emotionally. Abandoning such protections is essentially hurting yourself for nothing. "Should you?" I asked, an implicit admonishment and rejection of this idea.

But Komachi cutely tilted her head. "Hmm, the kind of person Komachi would like would probably not cheat...more like a weirdly conscientious *hinedere*. I don't think I'd have to worry."

"...Does a guy like that even exist?" *Don't be dumb, Komachi... I mean, this nonsensical "weirdly conscientious* hinedere*" guy can't be worth it. Pick someone better.*

"You'd be surprised." Komachi gave a shy and bashful smile but then immediately switched over to her usual high energy. "Okay, at last, the final competition!" she called loudly, and finally, the last round of the heart-fluttering brideness showdown was at hand.

Seriously, what even is brideness?

X X X

They made me wait for quite some time in the home ec room, so I was sitting there all zoned out.

It seemed Totsuka had slipped out from his club practice during a break, so he had to leave. He seemed disappointed he couldn't see the wedding dresses at the end, but it was nothing compared with the heartbreak I felt when I realized I couldn't see Totsuka in a wedding dress… Though actually, for this, I wouldn't mind him in a tux, either! In fact, I want to see that!

As I was voicelessly venting to myself, the door slid open noisily, and Komachi came in. Looking over, I saw she was wearing a wedding dress.

It wasn't the orthodox style—more of a miniskirt, and instead of pure-white fabric, it was yellow. The whole thing was a bit aggressive— healthy, bright, and distinctly cute.

Just like the impression the dress color gave, Komachi was even more worked up than before. "It's the joyful and embarrassing bridal outfit showdown~! Komachi even put on a different color. Bro, look, look!"

"Yeah, yeah, you're the cutest in the world," I said.

Komachi's shoulders slumped, and the energy in her voice flagged. "There it is, the Hachiman apathy. Well, whatever. So first, we start with Yui," Komachi said toward the door, an announcement followed by the timid sound of the door sliding open.

Yuigahama poked her face inside for a nervous peek, but then she seemed to steel herself and come in.

The fabric of her dress was pinkish and eye-catching, and it went well with her hair color. Her mini-length skirt puffed out, drawing attention to her surprisingly slender legs. The skirt pulled in tight at her waist, and the revealing bodice sparkled with dazzling sequins and lamé. Frankly, it was hard to look straight at it.

Maybe she was nervous, or maybe she was just unused to wearing something like this, as she walked in an awkward and stilted manner. She must have been genuinely embarrassed about the dress; when her eyes met mine, her cheeks reddened.

You're gonna infect me with your embarrassment, so could you stop glancing at me…?

Finally, she came up beside Komachi, then circled around behind her using the younger girl as her shield. "Um…K-Komachi-chan, where did this come from?"

"Eh-heh, that's a secret! ♪" Komachi dodged the question with a wink. She must have borrowed it from some sponsor bridal company. My little sister never overlooks anything.

"All righty then, next is Yukino!" Komachi called her name, and the door opened without a sound.

Yukinoshita came in so softly, even her footsteps made no sound.

Everyone held their breath.

The flowing contours of her pure-white dress emphasized the lines of her body. The flower decorations at her chest gave her a strong presence, and the gentle curves splayed out at her feet in lustrous fashion, like the fins of a mermaid. A long lace veil hung from her head like a sprinkling of snow lying on her jet-black hair. It enveloped her gently, not hiding her pale white skin but rather bringing out its glow.

Behind the veil, Yukinoshita closed her eyes and walked slowly forward, her face tilted slightly downward.

"...Why me, too?" I could hear her muttering.

It seemed she was quite angry. Though you couldn't see her properly, you could tell from her aura. You really could. Suddenly, her veil fluttered up a bit, and I got a peek of her displeased and embarrassed blush.

"Ohhh, she's mad... You can't hide the real Yukinoshita, even with a veil..."

"...What?" I could feel her gaze stabbing at me like a cold knife, even through the veil. You know, when a bride wears a white kimono, she has a *tsuno-kakushi* to cover the horns of any jealous demons she harbors; I wonder if the veil on a wedding dress is supposed to have a similar effect? It didn't seem to be working on Yukinoshita, though.

Once Yukinoshita was lined up beside Yuigahama, Komachi took in the sight of the two of them with satisfaction. Only one person was left in this bridal costume showdown.

"And now time for the leading lady~, Miss Hiratsukaaa~ ♪," Komachi called cheerfully, sounding somewhat more careless than she had with the last two. The way she was saying it, Miss Hiratsuka was less a leading lady and more like a pleading lady.

But regardless of Komachi's gentle call, the door gently and slowly opened. Instantly, silence fell over the room as everyone forgot to breathe.

A beautiful woman slowly entered the home ec room, closed her eyes gracefully, and took one step at a time so as to avoid treading on her long, flowing veil. When she passed in front of Komachi, even the girl who had called her in was left frozen in shock.

"...Who's that?" That was all a stunned Komachi managed to say. Oh, I was thinking exactly the same thing, though...

Her straight black hair was tied up in a somewhat high ponytail. Fine lace drifted down from her updo over her open back, but not enough to conceal the beauty of the curve from the back of her neck to her shoulder blades.

The dress itself was orthodox, somewhat classical in style, and it brought out the beauty of every part of her: the pure-white gloves on her shapely, thin, long fingers, the long skirts spreading out from her slim waist, and the simple decorations of the strapless dress emphasizing the fineness of her skin and ample bust.

"M-Miss Hiratsuka. You're beautiful...," said Yuigahama.

"Why couldn't you just be like this normally...?" Yukinoshita echoed.

Even girls could sense it, apparently. Both of them spoke in surprise and wonder.

"How about it, Hikigaya? Not bad, huh?" Miss Hiratsuka spun around to face me, a smug grin rising on her lips. That guileless smile, as if she'd just pulled off some mischievous prank, was the piece missing from the ensemble, and it fit perfectly into place.

I should have given at least one tactful response, but I just stared in a trance. When I realized I hadn't said anything, I scratched my cheek in an attempt to hide my embarrassment.

"U-uh...well...um...it's pretty," I said.

Miss Hiratsuka blinked a bunch. "...O-oh, you think? ... Th-thanks," she muttered, burying her face in the bouquet in her hands. It was cute to see her go red all the way to her ears—and very unlike someone of her age.

Man, seriously—why can't she get married…?

Yuigahama, Yukinoshita, and Miss Hiratsuka all lined up, and this concluded the bridal costume showdown. Now that the final round was done, Komachi called out "Announcing the results!" with a clap. So we clapped with her in a sparse semblance of applause.

Komachi nodded in satisfaction and then looked all around the home ec room. Her eyes landed on the dishes piled in the sink, the boards and dry erase markers, and the girls in the dresses. "Aw, you guys were all kinda pretty bad! …Guess the winner is Koma—"

"…"

Or so she started to say, when someone shot her an intense look. I felt a fierce will that prevented her from continuing, and I looked over toward the source of the unusually powerful energy to see Miss Hiratsuka glaring real death at her.

But Komachi attempted to keep going anyway. "Th-the winner is…"

"…"

In an attempt to escape the eyes still locked on her, Komachi turned away from Miss Hiratsuka. Sweat was rising on her forehead. "The… winner…is…"

"…!"

The intimidation was so thick that Komachi recoiled, shoulders shrinking away. With a weak, barely audible voice, she continued. "Th-the winner is…Miss Hiratsuka…," she whimpered brokenly, and Miss Hiratsuka gave a brilliant smile.

Wow, she looks so happy…

"Hmm? R-really? Oh, ah-ha-ha-ha! I can't believe I won! I guess marriage is on my horizon…," she crowed with shameless abandon, while Yuigahama forced a *ta-ha-ha* laugh and Yukinoshita gave a brief, exasperated sigh.

Komachi ran up to me, wailing and sniffling with tears in her eyes. "Th-that was scary… It was so scary…"

"There, there…" I petted Komachi's head, and as I calmed her, it hit me. *Oh yeah, I guess this is why Miss Hiratsuka is still single…*

Miss Hiratsuka seemed to be the only one thrilled with this result.

Watching her, Yuigahama seemed to be hit with an idea, as she suddenly clapped her hands. "Oh, since we're all dressed up, let's take a picture!" she suggested.

"Oh, that's a good idea! Here, Bro." Komachi instantly broke into a smile.

I knew it was crocodile tears, but your brother wishes you would try a little harder with those lies, okay...?

She prodded me in the back to get me moving for the picture.

"Don't push me..."

I was shoved in front of the window where the setting sun was just starting to shine in, and Yukinoshita smoothly stepped aside to avoid me. I think she meant to keep going and slip out of the picture entirely. "I'll sit this one out," she said.

But Yuigahama was waiting ahead, ready for her. "Come on, you too, Yukinon."

"Don't cling to me..."

Yuigahama just dragged Yukinoshita into the middle, then tugged me close by the sleeve.

"Don't yank me..."

"Just come on!" Yuigahama smiled cheerfully and pulled on both Yukinoshita's and my arms even harder.

"I'm ready! We're taking the picture!" Komachi must have set an automated timer. Once she'd finished setting up for the photo with her cell phone camera, she leaped toward us.

"This sort of thing isn't so bad now and again, is it?" Miss Hiratsuka said kindly. Standing to the side, she gently put her hand on my shoulder.

Well, sometimes. Oh, I'll send the photo to Totsuka later.

As the dusk light poured into the home ec room, the shutter clicked.

$$\times \quad \times \quad \times$$

It was late Friday night, a few days after the brideness showdown. We'd finished dinner, my parents were already asleep, and it was just me and Komachi downstairs.

I was listening to Komachi in the kitchen doing dishes as I sank into the sofa, facing my laptop. I'd completely forgotten that I had to write the piece for our section of the community magazine. Tomorrow was the weekend, so I'd be able to keep working on this until pretty late at night.

I've heard that mammals were originally nocturnal. Being a mammal, I also become more active at night. Plus, I really like mammaries.

So they want me to do a write-up, but what even about? I wondered as I tackled the draft that I had still not even written one letter of. There was hardly any time left until the deadline. What had I been doing all this time, you ask? Oh, no, you just don't get it. It wasn't coming to me at all. Do you understand this feeling? I guess you wouldn't. I don't get it, either. I had to hurry up and write something, anything.

As I was writing and erasing and writing and erasing, my block got worse and worse. Each moment I worried about what I should write or what turn of phrase to use, my hands stopped. I started spending more time in the background playing *KanColle* than having my hands on the keyboard.

I guess this is as far as I can go today, huh...?

Right around the time I was about to give up, my cell phone rang from its spot on the table a little ways away. The *bzz, bzz* of the vibration told me it was a call. *Oh, but I'm kinda busy right now.*

When I ignored it, I heard the squeak of Komachi turning off the faucet, and then she came out of the kitchen, wiping her hands with a towel. On the way, she picked up my phone and tossed it at me. "Bro, your phone."

"Uh-huh." I clapped my hands together to catch it.

Well, now that she'd gone to the trouble of getting it for me, I had to answer it. I looked at the display to see the caller was Yuigahama. Though I could basically imagine what she would say, I answered, holding the phone on my shoulder and continuing to work. "Hello?"

"Oh, Hikki, are you done?"

As I predicted, she was pressing me on the draft. *I said I'd send it to you once I'm done...* "It's not gonna get done just like that. Are you done with your part?"

"Yeah, I've drawn the pictures. Yukinon is gonna put every-thing together. So then once we have your draft, we'll be done." Yukinoshita was doing the editing work, and Yuigahama was drawing up some clip art. The division of labor had been matched to each of our aptitudes.

Hold on. If they're waiting for my draft, that's, like, way too much pressure. It's just gonna make me write slower... I fell apologetically silent for a moment, and I heard a faint voice on the other side.

"Is he done yet?"

That sounded like Yukinoshita. *Oh, so Yuigahama's staying over at Yukinoshita's place or something? How nice, you're such good friends...*

"Huh? Oh yeah. We were wondering if you're done yet." I could still hear Yuigahama's voice clearly. The phone must have been picking up Yukinoshita from a distance.

"Not yet."

"He says not yet. Huh? Okay, I'll ask." It sounded like Yuigahama was talking with Yukinoshita. There was another little pause before she replied to me. "She's asking when you'll be done."

"I don't know...and, like, this middleman thing is annoying." *We don't need to be playing a literal game of telephone here...*

After I said that, I could faintly hear a conversation on the other end: "Could I speak with him?" and "Oh, okay."

"Hello?"

"Hey."

Yukinoshita came onto the phone. Come to think of it, this might have been the first time I'd spoken with her on the phone.

As my mind wandered, Yukinoshita was getting straight to the point. "When will you be done?" Her tone, chilly as always, made me wince. Even over the phone, it has a weight that won't let you argue.

"I-it'll be this week..." I stuttered just a little from the guilt of being the only one behind schedule, and from the other side of the phone, I heard a short sigh.

"Today is Friday. If you're saying this week, can I take that to mean today? Do you know when the deadline is?"

"M-Monday morning..."

"That means next week. I'll just leave your space open and move things along. Once you're done, send what you've got to me."

"Yeah. Oh, but if I'm sending it—"

"Bye." Without waiting for me to finish, she hung up, leaving me with nothing but the dial tone in my ears.

I glared at the phone and muttered to myself, "...I can't send it if I don't even know your e-mail address."

So no matter how I tried, it seemed the draft could not be submitted until Monday. There was no helping it. It was Yukinoshita's fault for not listening to me properly... Well, about as much as it was mine for not sticking to the deadline.

Having survived the pressure from the phone call for the time being, I was now at ease and breathed a short sigh. Tossing away my phone, I rotated my shoulders.

I still hadn't bought myself much time, though. *This is a pain, so let's get it done fast.*

I was going to battle my computer once more, when a cup of coffee was gently offered to me. Looking up, I saw Komachi standing there with two cups.

I took one thankfully, and she sat down beside me. Guess she intended to stay awake here with me.

"You don't have to wait for me or anything," I said. I didn't know how long this would take. Maybe all night.

Komachi gave a little shake of her head. "No, I want to read anyway, so I'll wait."

Well, tomorrow's the weekend, so she can stay up a little later. "...Do what you want," I said, taking a sip of coffee and then starting to hit the keyboard again.

When you're working alone, it's easy to just start slacking, but when someone is there right beside you waiting, it forces you to work harder.

Fighting to finish even a little earlier, I desperately strung together some half-assed BS, building up my page count and hours spent. The keys clacked away in the silence of the night. The only other thing I could hear was the occasional drip of water from the sink.

At some point, very, very soft sounds of snoozing joined them.

I finished writing most of the piece, and once I had only a little more to go, I looked beside me to see Komachi just nodding off to sleep. Her comfortable weight gently leaning on my shoulder made me close my eyes, just for an instant.

But only an instant.

As the final line rose in my mind, I typed it slowly, so as not to wake her.

Be it marriage or your future path in life, you can never know what's coming. And even if you prepare yourself, there will always be new troubles awaiting you.

But everyone has the right to wish for happiness.

You can't slack in your preparations for the times to come. Conclusion: Women, you should nab those promising househusbands as soon as possible.

Short Story 2
Of course, **Hachiman Hikigaya**'s kindness is contrary.

Fall continued onward, and the leaves were turning color here and there. The season was showing signs of change, however gradual. And something a little strange had happened here in the Service Club recently, too.

"The Chiba Prefecture–Wide Advice E-mail!" Yuigahama did this weird announcement of the title, all excited, for some reason. "Duh-duh-duh-duuuuh!" she added with a round of solo applause. Yukinoshita's and my eyes were cold.

This was our recent little anomaly. Miss Hiratsuka had suddenly gotten it in her head to give the Service Club a new assignment, and this was to respond to requests for advice sent to us from wherever via e-mail.

Maintaining the same level of enthusiasm, Yuigahama continued, reading out an e-mail. "Okay then, our first e-mail today is from someone living in Chiba city and calling themselves: I'm anxious."

Does this person not know what *username* means? That sounds like it should be the title. They strike me as the type of person who won't read the instructions fully when it clearly says *Please read the instructions fully*. Eugh, why bother giving advice or anything to someone who can't stick to the rules? I'm not very keen on this.

```
Request for advice from username: I'm anxious
```

The older students have retired, so I'm going to be captain of the tennis club. What should I do to get everyone to follow my lead? Please tell me if there's anything I should watch out for. Thank you.

...Oh-ho, I see. He mistook the username section for the title and ended up writing a title in there instead. How cute. Oh geez, to make such a minor, cute little slipup, he must be very anxious indeed. How very adorable.

"Okay, I'm gonna answer this good!" I declared.

"You're awfully keen to help all of a sudden..."

I ignored Yuigahama's surprise and exasperation and moved on so as to resolve this pressing issue as soon as possible. "Well, first, you're a club captain, too, Yukinoshita. What do you think?"

"...Yes, well, if my personal thoughts on the matter would be sufficient..." Yukinoshita had been reading her book disinterestedly, but when she was specifically called upon, as you might expect, she closed her book and adopted a thinking pose. "The first step of taking control is displaying your own merits. Once you're standing on top, employ suppression, informants, and a thorough purge of the opposition. Then, within a brief year or so, you should be able to solidify your regime," she said, with a great big smile.

That grin really is terrifying, you know...

"Hmm, but would that actually work out?" said Yuigahama. "It sounds good when you call it *leadership*, but if you go too far, I think that just makes people resent you."

"Yeah, that's true," I agreed. "A certain club captain around here seems less invested in showing leadership and more in acting arbitrarily on her own authority and throwing her weight around. *And* nobody likes her."

"Could you not say that while looking at me...?" Yukinoshita was sullen. Maybe she was actually aware of what she's like and was worried about it, in her own way.

...If you're worried about it, then fix it.

"W-well, there are lots of different kinds of leaders!" Yuigahama said, attempting to mediate, and she began typing out a reply to the e-mail.

```
Response from the Service Club:
A club captain doesn't just stand at the front and
drag people behind them. I think maybe you could be
the kind of captain who relies on the support of their
club members. If you push too hard, they might be put
off, so be careful. You can do it!
```

Yeah, that settles that one.

Starting on the next one, Yuigahama said, "Um, the next e-mail is...from someone living in Chiba city, with the username: Master Swordsman General."

Him again... It's like we have a regular. It's actually kinda flattering, which is why it needs to stop.

```
Request for advice from username: Master Swordsman
General
I've heard tell online that for light-novel new-
bie awards these days, anyone who can write Japanese
will make it through the first round, but 'tis not so.
Source: I. Instruct me on how to make it.
```

After reading that e-mail, Yukinoshita looked confused. "Perhaps we should begin with correcting the Japanese in this e-mail..."

"What's he saying? I can't even," Yuigahama said.

When it comes to Japanese level, I think you're probably about the same, though.

"Basically, his question is, how can he win a newcomer's award and get published?" I explained, then glanced over at Yuigahama with the implication I was seeking her opinion.

But she just grimaced. "Huh? This one is yours, Hikki. You answer."

Yukinoshita agreed and nodded, too. "I believe being harsh can be a form of kindness." Having said what she wanted to say, Yukinoshita dropped her gaze to the paperback in her hands and went back to reading.

Hmm. Then maybe something like this. I pulled the computer close to me and typed a message.

```
Response from the Service Club:
If the readers and editing department staff won't
acknowledge you, it's their problem. Have confidence
and never change. Never give up, keep on chasing your
dreams, right until your end, forever and ever.
```

Satisfied at finishing my response, I let slip a sigh of satisfaction. The trick here is making it *your end* instead of *the end.*

"Ohhh, you're so nice, Hikki."

"…Kindness can be so cruel."

Yuigahama, peeking at the screen, was innocently startled, while Yukinoshita lowered her gaze sadly and softly.

Well, let's say kindness is a double-edged sword.

SS
2

Bonus track!
"Komachi Hikigaya's Plot."

This bonus track is a novelization of the script from the limited special edition drama CD *Komachi Hikigaya's Plan*, from a *My Youth Romantic Comedy Is Wrong, As I Expected* event. The script features an episode set immediately after Volume 3 of the main series as well as the bonus track *Like, This Sort of Birthday Song*.

Were we not born to play? Were we not born for fun?

So it is written in the songs of old in *Ryojin Hisho*. But is fun the raison d'être of humanity? If it is, then life is play itself, and everything in life is a game.

Be that as it may, we don't know exactly what the words *play* or *fun* refer to here. The words mean a wide variety of things; these are vaguely defined terms.

For example, "Hey, hey, let's have some fun, honey," makes me think, *Go and die, normie*, while "You were just playing with me, weren't you?!" makes me *really* think, *Go and die, normie*.

If you play around too much when you're cooking, it'll generally turn into a disaster, and when you try something and fail at it, it's common to excuse yourself by saying "Oh, that was just for fun."

In other words, play is nothing but trouble.

But on the other hand, if the goal of life is to have fun and fun is nothing but trouble, then life is nothing but trouble.

Ryojin Hisho is impressive indeed, to so accurately predict the awful fates of people who play around. Emperor Go-Shirakawa went bald for a reason. It was probably all those tribulations that did it. He should be ranked up there with Bruce Willis and Nicholas Cage as one of the top three coolest bald guys in the world. I think instead of implanting hair, we should be implanting the idea that baldness is a cool status symbol.

Anyway, to sum up, the pros and cons of the terms *fun*, or *play*, as well as the behavior they refer to, should be called into question.

What will become of you if you do nothing but play around? That tragic eventuality is not difficult to imagine.

But if you pore over the history on the subject, you discover "a Gadabout can change classes to Sage at level 20."

So then, well, you know…maybe it's fine for me to play around a little bit…

$$\times \quad \times \quad \times$$

It wasn't like we planned it or anything, but we ended up throwing a birthday party for Yuigahama.

There was Yuigahama, Yukinoshita, Totsuka, who joined us on the way, and Komachi, who was waiting for us there. Plus, we decided to take along Zaimokuza for the sake of altruism. With me in the party as well, we all went to karaoke, and there I witnessed something I never should have seen.

Our thirtyish teacher had been driven out of a matchmaking party and had come to karaoke alone to kill time. Yeah, that'd make you sing about some heartbreak…the melancholy strains of an *enka* ballad…

When this thirtyish matchmaking-party-leaving *enka*-singing teacher had found us, she'd let out a cry of grief and run off.

The humidity of the rainy season air abated at sunset, and the wind blowing toward the sea was cool. A wail of sorrow rode that wind to my ears.

"I want to get married…"

This longing, so simple and basic, echoed through the town at night.

I don't know if it was that Doppler effect or whatever you call it

I
want
to
get
married…

(PaRappa effect?), but that voice strangely stuck in my ears. In fact, it even made my eyes misty and created pain in my chest. What the heck, does her voice work like mustard gas?

It seemed I wasn't the only one feeling chest pains, as all eyes shifted in the direction Miss Hiratsuka had disappeared.

We were speechless. But then Totsuka, the most decent human being of the group, spoke up with concern. "M-Miss Hiratsuka ran off crying... I wonder if she's okay...?"

As expected of Totsuka. He's so kind. He really is. It was so incredibly kind of him to let me see that hesitant timidity as he peered off toward the corner where Miss Hiratsuka had turned.

The reply was less kind—cold as ice, in fact. "She's old enough, so I figure she's all right," Yukinoshita said calmly, lightly sweeping her hair back.

If she would just keep her mouth shut, she'd be easy on the eyes, too... But she wasn't exactly wrong. In fact, she was too right. I found myself agreeing with her. "I guess. In fact, age-wise, she's more than old enough."

Seriously, she really is more than old enough—so please, someone, take her soon.

"Herm, a brave declaration, such that fears not death... Bravery is our birthright, lads!" Off to the side, Zaimokuza wiped sweat from his brow with a look of terror as he cried out with even more melodrama and...annoyingness.

"Well anyway, the party was fun, huh?" Komachi casually sidestepped his weighty declaration. As expected of the Hikigaya household's ultimate communication weapon. She smoothly ignored Zaimokuza himself, a man who anyone else would hesitate to deal with.

Then Yuigahama smiled brightly, employing her constantly-checking-up-on-everyone-style communication skills. "Thanks so much for today, Komachi-chan. You guys, too."

Komachi smiled back at her, and Yukinoshita, watching from a little ways away, also breathed a gentle sigh of relief. Well, she must have been trying to be thoughtful in her own way that day, too.

Thanks for your efforts. I figured shooting her a look of gratitude would ruin this nice good mood, so I kept that to myself.

As long as Yuigahama was satisfied, that was enough.

Plus, well, it wasn't like I was bored out of my mind the whole time, either.

"That was so fun, I lost track of time," Totsuka commented, which led Zaimokuza and me to both check our phone clocks.

"Herm, now that you mention it, 'tis already that time. The hour of darkness begins…" For some reason, Zaimokuza gazed off into the distant western sky, dyed crimson with the looming sunset. If I were to indulge him, we really would be here till the sun went down, though, so I casually ignored him.

"Uh-huh. I'm going, then. See you."

"Oh yeah. See you later." Yuigahama timidly waved good-bye, and I replied with a nonchalant raise of my hand.

But then in the corner of my eye, I saw Komachi. It seemed she was up to something, as she wriggled and creeped up to Yuigahama. "Light bulb! Yui!" When Komachi popped up there suddenly, Yuigahama let out a confused cry, then Komachi rattled on to her in a whisper.

And what is that girl planning…? I had a bad feeling tugging at me from behind, making it real hard to go. I walked away slowly, but I could hear little snatches of what Komachi was saying.

"You're okay with just going home now? I feel bad about saying this, as his little sister, but it's rare, superrare, for my brother to go out of the house at all… The next time he'll go out will be…*glance,*" she said in the most obvious way as she looked over at me.

Yuigahama seemed to be considering this, as her waving gradually slowed—and eventually stopped. "Wai… Wai… Wait. Wait!" Feet pattering against the ground, Yuigahama came up to me. "L-let's have some more fun!"

"Huh? There's a strict curfew at my house."

I will instantly refuse any invitation. This is a loner's standard move, as well as an evasive instinct. I mean, you know, if you say you'll go, and then it turns out they were just inviting you to be polite, and you get an *Oh, you're going...* with that strained smile like that time in middle school with the class party, then you'd feel bad, right? Meeting thoughtfulness with thoughtfulness is the courtesy of an adult.

But it seemed Yuigahama had not meant to be polite, and she turned to Komachi in order to verify my testimony. "Is that right, Komachi-chan?" she asked.

"No. There's nothing like that at our house." Komachi shook her head. Our house *is* the laissez-faire type. Well, more like our parents are busy, so they wouldn't be home yet.

Upon Komachi's reply, I heard the *phew* of a quiet sigh. "Telling a lie in front of your sister, knowing it'll be immediately exposed... I don't know whether to call it brash or brave... It's rare enough for someone to invite you out, so why not gracefully accept?" Yukinoshita said, exasperated.

But who's gonna want to go when you talk to them like that? How bad at invitations can you get?

"Uh, well, we have a cat at home," I answered. "I've gotta go home and take care of him."

A shoddy invitation gets a shoddy refusal.

Yukinoshita stopped in her tracks. Then she hesitated just a moment.

I could hear the meow of a cat—most likely from either my or Yukinoshita's brain.

She nodded with an *mm-hmm*. "I see. If it's for a cat, this is the only way."

"That convinced you?!" said Komachi. "Listen, the cat's fine! Y-you know, they say that pets resemble their owners, so I'm sure he's fine by himself!"

"Hey, you didn't need to add that last part." It's certainly true that both Komachi and I are not only fine being left alone—we kind of want you to keep your distance. But that kind of makes it sound like we can't function in society, or even like we're no longer human.

But Yuigahama did not listen to what I had to say at all. In fact, she was tug-tugging on Yukinoshita's sleeve and looking at me with moist eyes, too. "Come on, let's have some more fun! We're all going."

"When did we all decide to go...? Hey, does this include me?" Yukinoshita expressed her displeasure at finding the plan had been decided without her input.

But Yuigahama puffed out her chest as if this were completely obvious. "Of course!" she said emphatically.

Yukinoshita blinked, then tilted her face downward. "I—I see..."

Yukinoshita's muted and stuttering response must have puzzled Yuigahama, as she peered at Yukinoshita's face with some concern. "...You didn't want to?"

"I don't mean that... I'm just somewhat surprised." She raised her face again and shook her head a little. Her smooth, glossy black hair swayed slightly, covering her blushing cheeks.

But Yuigahama was right in front of her, so Yukinoshita probably couldn't hide her blush entirely. Yuigahama seemed captivated by that gesture, as she let out the slightest sigh.

...Oh no, Yukinoshita's completely fallen for her. These girlish lovers are a sight to behold, like a golden mosaic.

And then yet another white lily jumped into this *yuri*-licious scene. "So, so then I take it you can come, too, Yukino?! That'd be worth a lot of Komachi points!" Komachi brightly said to her.

Comparatively calmer, Yukinoshita replied, "Yes. This is Yuigahama, after all. So even if I were to refuse, I figure she would keep trying, so I won't cause a fuss. I'll come along."

"Yay! Then you come, too, Hikki!" Now with Yukinoshita on as an ally, Yuigahama was suddenly encouraged.

And then unexpected reinforcements came to her side. "Aye, Hachiman. Prepare thyself! If you go, then I...shall go!"

"You like me too much..."

I ended up on the receiving end of Zaimokuza's annoying love call. He's gotten a little too attached to me lately, and I'm scared...of myself, for being on the edge of acknowledging his existence.

But I am a man. I have my pride. I have my self-respect. I have my convictions.

I'm not going to recant what I've said that easily. A man does not go back on his word. If I said I don't want to do something, then I will absolutely never do it. Also, even if I have said I'll do something, whether or not I'll do it depends on the time and circumstances.

I could not have them misjudging me. I will pull out all the stops to make things easier on myself. This was why I would go so far as attempt to bullshit Yuigahama to get out of this.

"Listen, Yuigahama. What is *fun* anyway? If you live a vague, aimless life, you'll die a vague, aimless death. Are you okay with that?"

"Why are you lecturing me...?" Yuigahama made grumpy noises at me, but she should have been grateful that I hadn't even added any real punch to that lecture. Seeing the exasperation in her face, though, I supposed I'd pulled off a decent smoke screen.

During this moment of relief, Yukinoshita put her hand to her chin and lightly shook her head. "...You do have a point, though. Now that you mention it, the word *fun* is rather vague," she muttered, as if talking to herself.

Komachi stuck up her pointer finger and looked up into the air as she began to think. "Hmm, when you say *play*, like hide-and-seek or tag, it comes off nice and simple, which, in terms of Komachi points—"

"Points, points, points. Shut up. Are you a convenience store clerk? I didn't bring my card." Every time they ask me that, I don't have my card, and it makes me feel guilty. To make it worse, they might say, *Oh! That's fine,* but then the follow-up attack will be the kindly asked *Do you want to make a new one?* and then I end up replying, *Oh! I'm fine.* What the heck is that *Oh* even for? Is there, like, a rule where you have to put it before every word? It's like that one you always have to put before English nouns.

As I was indulging myself with trivial thoughts of this nature...

"And then there's color tag, and freeze tag, and high-safe tag... Um...and also..." Totsuka was earnestly folding down his fingers as he tried to remember. It sounded like he was trying to derive an answer to the question of *What is play?* by listing out every game. Coming up with examples and drawing commonalities in order to come up with the truth—truly a wonderful method. His slightly parted lips as he considered were cherubic. Truly wonderful.

So I decided to help, too. "Then there's cops and robbers, and robbers and cops, I guess."

Immediately, Yuigahama's mouth popped open in confusion. "Aren't those the same thing?" she asked.

What? Don't open your mouth like an idiot; I'll stick garbage in it. Just close your mouth—close it.

I gave her a squinty, rotten-eyed look, and Yukinoshita patted her on the shoulder. "Yuigahama, Hikigaya hasn't had much experience playing with other people, so he won't have been exposed to much variety. Please be considerate."

Now realizing that, Yuigahama apologized most sincerely. "Ah, o-oh... I-I'm sorry."

"Don't actually apologize to me like that. I don't want to face my past."

Also, Yukinoshita was acting like she was being all considerate of me, but that wasn't at all what was happening, you know? How could she say stuff like that with such a big smile on her face?

"But Bro, you never played outside at all." Komachi took the opportunity to bring up my youth as a rosy-cheeked young boy. Well, it's less rosy-cheeked and more red-faced shame, though...

"Shuddup, I'm a modern boy. I'm living in the future!"

Yukinoshita burst into a brilliant smile and said, as if that had quite convinced her, "Well, you need someone to play with in order to play the more active games outside. Oh, so that's why they called you Hikki? The name follows the nature, as they say. What a truly apt saying."

How sweet. She's about as sweet as MAX Coffee. Whoa, that's *really* sweet, though. I guess that'd be too sweet—maybe like gelato level. Hey, why the hell is canned MAX Coffee sweeter than actual sweets?

"Ha! Don't you underestimate loners. I can play active games all by myself."

"Yeah, yeah, Bro is always boxing with the string dangling from the ceiling bulb, or tossing three-point shots with his socks into the wash basket!"

Hey? Komachi-chan? Why are you telling people this? Look, Yukinoshita's starting to get exasperated, you know?

"He's doing it in the present continuous tense, huh…? How stupid can you be…?"

"I can't help it. Once you start, you just kinda get into it." In fact, it gets more fun over time. Recently, I've been pitching with my favorite socks. I've taken the mound as closer nine times, and lately, I've been amusing myself by imagining a scenario where I totally blank my opponents. By the way, my winning pitch is a knuckleball.

I considered explaining this to Yukinoshita in detail, but I could imagine the reaction I'd get if I did, so I dropped it. The one person who would probably understand—my sister, Komachi—did not seem interested in listening to what I had to say and was already moving on to the next topic.

"So that means wherever we go next, we'll get into it once we get started. Let's go, Bro!"

"Huh…?" I was getting a sneaking suspicion I'd been hoodwinked.

While I was still showing reluctance, Totsuka stepped up to me. "Um, I plan to go, so…I'd be glad if you were there, too, Hachiman."

"Okay, where are we going? What are we doing? I'll do anything that doesn't involve breaking the law!" *What?! Tell me that first! Suddenly, I'm starting to look forward to this!*

"Herm. He changes his mind with such speed… He is Super High-Speed Transforming… Despairingly cool!" Zaimokuza met my cheer with an aggressive thumbs-up. I nearly returned the gesture on reflex, but upon seeing Zaimokuza himself, I managed to stop myself. Thank you, Zaimokuza.

"I feel like I'm missing something, but I can't put my finger on it…" Yuigahama looked doubtful as she watched my exchange with Totsuka, but then she nodded and energetically clapped her hands. "…Anyway, now it's decided!"

By contrast, Yukinoshita tilted her head, making thinking noises. "But what do you suggest? At our age, playing tag or house really would be rather absurd."

"It's not that weird. Normies are all basically playing house in the classroom." They decide what roles they'll be playing and interact according to the expectations of those roles, just like playing house. I guess you can be happy enough if you're not aware you're doing it, but once you can see the template of these conversations, of this way of life, it just gets sad. You have to bear that awareness your whole life. The only people you can share that feeling with are the others who have it themselves, but that very awareness makes it difficult to coexist with them.

Yukinoshita, who could probably understand this as well as I did, cracked a smile. "My, that way of putting it fits you perfectly. Someone who's always playing hide-and-seek in the classroom will have a different eye for things."

"I suppose. I've always been real good at hide-and-seek, you know. I'm so good that back in elementary school, I'd be hiding the whole time until everyone else went home."

"A tragic talent..." Yukinoshita put her hand to her temple and breathed an exasperated sigh.

See? We really can't coexist.

But Yuigahama was even worse. "But, Hikki, the classroom doesn't really hide you? Actually, when you're all alone, you just stick out in a bad way."

"I'm surrounded by so many its... I really am..."

But even though they're supposed to be it, none of them ever find me... Hachiman knows. All of Class 2-F are good friends! Except me.

"I-it's okay, Hachiman. I'm here, too, now. So let's just decide where we're going to hang out? Okay?"

Found you, Hachiman! I could almost hear it as an angel desce— Oh, my mistake. That was just Totsuka talking. He was so pure, I was about to rise up to heaven...

"Herm, if no one else has any ideas, then the arcade would be splendid. This is my super-top number-one recommendation."

As I was zoning out, I got the feeling someone had made a pompous suggestion...but anyway, Totsuka was right—we had to think of a place to go.

"So what are we gonna do?" I brought up the topic again.

Komachi had been deep in thought, and her hand suddenly shot up as if she'd just hit on an idea. "Oh! An arcade! Yeah, we could do that, couldn't we? Okay, Komachi's on board with the arcade!"

"Oh yeah, it's close by. And last time I went with you, Hachiman, we weren't able to play many games." Totsuka agreed with Komachi, and I agreed with him.

"Okay, Totsuka. If that's what you want, then let's go with the arcade. And no one is allowed to argue."

It seemed Yukinoshita and Yuigahama had no particular objections, as both of them nodded.

"Hmm? Hmm~? This is rather odd~? I was the one who just said that~?" Zaimokuza was at the back all alone, muttering to himself, but we just told him not to worry about it and pushed him along as we set off to the nearby arcade.

Right, the arcade with Totsuka! I hope we can do *purikura* again!

X   X   X

Ah, the arcade.

It's a familiar hangout for high school kids. The loud noise keeps you from being bothered by the chattering of couples or groups of friends, and you can lose yourself in the crowd and feel you're alone, which gives you some degree of internal peace. Thanks to the noise, everyone has an equal place here. It's a venue that can put the heart of someone like me at relative ease.

"This place is so loud... So what should we do here?"

This must have been new to Yukinoshita, as she was glancing around. Yeah, when we went to the LaLaport mall before, that arcade was more family oriented. It was more light, more poppy, more amusement-centric, so this was probably the first time she had come to a real *arcade*, with all the clamor and tobacco smoke.

"Let's start by looking around a bit," I said. There was no point in just standing there and staring off into space. I prompted the others, and we went in to look.

As we were strolling around, Yuigahama noticed something and pointed. "Oh, that looks kinda fun."

"Ohhh, that's neat." Komachi looked at what Yuigahama was pointing at. "*Mah-jongg Fight Club*, huh?"

"Wow, so you can play with anyone in the country online."

With games these days, everything is all networked. I wish they would be more considerate of those people who don't have enough friends to make a collection, or those who try to turn over a new leaf and still end up living in a tent without a place to call home.

"How about it? Do you want to try playing mah-jongg, Komachi-chan?" asked Yuigahama.

"Yeah! I'll play you in national-tournament mode, Yui!"

"Don't. I think you guys'd be supergood, so don't." Also, I think Yukinoshita's sister, Haruno, would be loved by the tiles, and Kawa-something seems like she'd be supergood at digital style. I bet they'd all be good at mah-jongg...

Unaware of these opinions of mine, Yukinoshita gazed at the mah-jongg game cabinet from a distance and muttered, "Is mah-jongg a feminine game? I've never gotten that impression."

"Yeah, it does come off like a man's game, huh? It's so masculine and cool..." Just as Totsuka said, maybe it was easier to imagine men playing mah-jongg. Like on the night of the school field trip, all the boys' rooms had had mah-jongg tables set up.

Similarly, I play a bit of mah-jongg myself. Well, I say that, but I just know the hands. I can't calculate the scores, I don't know anything about tactics, and I don't have anyone to play with, either. But the computer serves as my opponent, so that doesn't trouble me.

Then I found my eyes moving toward a familiar arcade cabinet. Komachi perceptively caught the line of my eye and smirked. "Oh, that's the mah-jongg game you always play, isn't it, Bro? The one where they take off their uniforms if you win."

"Hey, you jerk, shut up. Don't talk about that now. Totsuka'll hear."

Don't you go slandering your big brother, insinuating that he plays indecent games like that. What if that made Totsuka hate me, and he started blushing a little and saying shyly, *N-nothing you can do about that, huh? Y-you're a boy, after all, Hachiman...*? I'd either want to die or maybe discover I enjoy the twisted thrill of imagining myself throwing uncensored porn at a cute girl who still believes in cabbage patches and storks.

Fortunately, it seemed Totsuka had not heard that.

I was breathing a sigh of relief when Yukinoshita's voice attacked me like a spray of ice water down my back. "...Be a little more considerate of us." I didn't know if she was angry or exasperated, but it sure was a glare. Scary!

My fearful gaze swept away from her and ended up instead on Yuigahama, who was beckoning me over with little hand gestures. "Oh, but look, look, it seems like women often do it, too... Wait... Huh...?" Following Yuigahama's pointing, I looked over and saw someone surrounded by a familiar air of sorrow.

"Oh, luck's on my side today! At least the mah-jongg tiles like me. *Why* don't men like me? I can go out in mah-jongg, but not on a date... Ha-ha-ha...hah..." Her deep sigh brought with it a cloud of tobacco smoke that obscured her face, but there was no mistaking that figure.

"It's...Miss...Hira...tsuka..." Yuigahama said her name timidly, as if to make absolutely sure.

Apparently, after Miss Hiratsuka had fled from us, she'd ended up sulking and playing mah-jongg in this arcade, with nowhere else to go. Zaimokuza put a hand to his chest and stood tall as if mourning, while Totsuka sadly looked down.

A heavy and somewhat tragic mood hung heavy over the area, at odds with the cheery environs.

Whoa, I don't wanna call out to her...

While I was waffling as to whether I should just ignore it or talk to her, Yukinoshita pushed me in the back. "Go on. She's your homeroom teacher."

"Don't push me. And wait, could you please not make this my job?"

When did that get decided? *If I go take care of her this once, it'll keep going and eventually become a thing, and that's the last thing I want, okay?*

As we were having this exchange, from behind I heard some sort of mumbling. "A sorrowful single teacher… Ha! That works! That works in Komachi terms, too! It's best to have as many candidates as possible…"

I turned around to see Komachi folding down fingers as she counted something. And then, once she'd arrived at her conclusion, she shot her hand up and stepped forward. "You just leave this to Komachi!" Before she even finished talking, she was already zooming over to Miss Hiratsuka's side.

"She ran off with a big smile on her face…"

Just as Yukinoshita said, there was a great mischievous grin on her face, one I knew all too well. "Things never end well when she's got that smile on…"

"Oh, I think I got that…" Yuigahama gave an awkward *ta-ha*.

Sorry my little sister is always causing you trouble. "Right? …Well, I do have to admit it's cute, though."

"Here comes the sister-complex…," Yuigahama said with exasperation.

That's not it, though. It's not a sister-complex—I just love her.

Said beloved little sister quietly sneaked up behind Miss Hiratsuka and then called out to her in the cheeriest tone. "Teacher! ♪"

"Hmm? Wh-whoa, oh, H-Hikigaya's sister… I-is something up?" Miss Hiratsuka must not have been expecting anyone to speak to her. Her back snapped rigidly, sending her stool scraping across the floor. The line of her back drew a pretty arch that made you imagine the supple muscles there. This has nothing to do with the current situation, but I think arching backs are superhot.

My little sister, knowing nothing of her brother's heart (though the opposite is also true), drew closer to Miss Hiratsuka, brought her hands together in entreaty, and began her eloquent explanation. "Oh, no, not at all. We just happened to be hanging out here right now, and we were wondering if you wouldn't mind coming with us. Well, actually, I was figuring we might need someone to keep an eye on my brother…"

"Uh… Uh-huh. W-well, if that's what's going on… I can handle that," Miss Hiratsuka agreed readily. Komachi's smooth talk must have gotten to her.

Watching their exchange at a distance, Yukinoshita suddenly breathed a little sigh. "It seems they've come to an agreement."

"All right, one more time, then: Let's have a blast!" Yuigahama said, then rushed over to Miss Hiratsuka and Komachi. Totsuka trotted, while Zaimokuza barreled over like a juggernaut.

Yukinoshita and I, the only two left, gave each other a look, sighed a little, then decided to meekly go with the flow.

✕   ✕   ✕

We took an aimless look around the arcade.

In the dim light, the luminescent screens were harsh on our eyes as character voices reached our ears occasionally over the blaring background music. One fanfare rang out particularly loud.

"Hey, how about it! *Shining Star Horse*, the horse-racing game!" And then there was Zaimokuza, whose voice was no less blaring.

Maybe his yelling was why I made the mistake of mumbling a perfunctory response. "A horse-racing game, huh...?"

"Oh, you don't sound enthusiastic about that one. I thought the conventional wisdom was that deadbeat men love to gamble," Miss Hiratsuka said, looking surprised.

"I've made the conscious decision not to gamble. And hey, I'm not a deadbeat..." *My grades are decent enough, and in class, I act quiet and serious, you know?* Well, that's because there's no one for me to talk to. That makes group discussions in English sketch. What's sketch about it, you ask? The person beside me will immediately start fiddling with their cell phone—that's what's sketch about it. At least check with me first? Ask it like, *We don't actually have to do this, right?* Well, it's sketch when you hear that, too, huh? All I've been saying here is sketch; man, never mind English, even my Japanese is sketch.

I get the feeling that I'm less a deadbeat and more a failure all around.

It seemed I was not the only one to think that, as Yukinoshita suddenly gave me a disparaging smile. "In your case, your lifestyle itself is a gamble, isn't it? The odds there seem extreme."

"Don't you lowball my odds of winning at life. Being a house-husband is a supersafe bet as a life goal."

"That's a real gamble..." Yuigahama muttered her frank impression with a shudder.

No, it's not... I just haven't met The One yet, that's all...

Yeah, it's not my fault. Fate's at fault here.

"So maybe something like that would be nice?"

That? You mean the one for me? I thought, but it was Totsuka. He was pointing at a medal game cabinet. It was one of those things where you insert some medals, and more pay out. Not the ones they have at candy stores where you win medals from playing rock-paper-scissors; one of those gizmos they call pusher machines, where the medals get pushed off a ledge and fall down.

These games are fairly intuitive to play, so you wouldn't have that much trouble trying to operate them. You often see couples playing these things.

Put another way, the game is for the casual customer base.

Perhaps this was why Zaimokuza cleared his throat with a *kehpum* noise and said smugly, "Herm, medal games, huh? Such trivial fare! I derive no pleasure from such shallow and juvenile contraptions!"

"So basically, this is a game where you insert a medal to make the accumulated medals fall out? How incredibly simplistic." Yukinoshita must also have seen this as a game for kids. She sounded less than interested.

"Oh, come on, everyone should give it a shot once. Simpler games are actually easier to get into," Miss Hiratsuka interjected with a wry smile.

Well, this is one of those things you really do have to try yourself.

$\times$ $\times$ $\times$

The roar of the arcade cabinets practically drowned out the faint background music of the building. In the distance, I could hear the voices of some excited young people.

And then there was the medal game cabinet in front of us, where the little coins clinked in a lively dance.

Despite the din around us, it felt quiet here, probably because none of us were talking.

"…"

"…"

At some point, even Zaimokuza and Yukinoshita, after all their arrogance before, had gone silent. But their eyes were in constant motion, their fingers always searching for the right moment to insert a medal.

"Ah! Awww, that was close. Ngh~. Why didn't that knock it down?"

"Quiet, Yuigahama."

I think you're just getting too into this… This seems kinda awkward for Yuigahama; I'm feeling sorry for her, you know?

There was another sorry individual here, too.

"…Herm. Don't underestimate the power of the evil eye… I can see it! Ah, ahem…missed… Ngh, the image remains in my eyes…"

"You can't see it at all, can you…?" I sighed. With this one, it's his brain that's the sorry part. *Also, didn't you just call it kids' stuff? You're totally enjoying it.*

But Zaimokuza wasn't the only one having fun.

"…Ngh, I can't believe I missed the jackpot…" Yukinoshita was the type to get worked up over competition in any form, as she was so focused I was sure she was on the verge of punching the machine. What's more, she was so quick to pick things up, she'd been raking it in…

"Y-you guys are all so serious…," said Totsuka. "Yukinoshita figured out the rules at some point, too."

"This has gotten kind of intense…," Komachi agreed.

The two of them, who had been enjoying this in a healthier way, had paused to watch with some dismay. But Yukinoshita and Yuigahama, fixated on the medal games as they were, didn't even notice as they continued to play.

"Ah, Yukinon. I'm borrowing some medals." Yuigahama reached out a hand, but Yukinoshita grabbed it tight.

"Stop right there. Do you have any hope of actually returning them? You've been tossing in medal after medal without a plan."

"Urk…" Yuigahama froze up after she heard Yukinoshita's point. It was true she'd been spending them like water. She was one of those people you needed to keep far away from gambling.

Yukinoshita seemed to be of the same opinion, as she stuck up her index finger and earnestly lectured Yuigahama. "And I've been telling you for quite some time now that you're distinctly lacking in foresight…"

"Uuuurk…" With every word, Yuigahama cringed away harder. And Yukinoshita was right, so nobody could help Yuigahama.

Foresight is important.

"Komachi, give me some medals," I said.

"You're not even going to pretend you're borrowing them? That's just like you, Bro…" She was beyond exasperated, but there was a kind of enlightened understanding in her expression.

Come on, if I can't return them anyway, then it's correct for me to say "give"! I'm just being honest! I was trying to use sibling telepathy to tell Komachi this with my eyes when there came a voice from the arcade cabinet behind us.

"You wanted some, Hikigaya?" There was a jangle as Miss Hiratsuka offered me some medals.

I reached out my hand like, *Yay! Jackpot!* But Komachi slapped my hand away.

Come on, Miss Hiratsuka said it's fine, so what's the big deal? I thought, giving her a grumpy look.

But Komachi wagged a scolding finger at me, then turned around to Miss Hiratsuka. "Um, could you please not spoil my brother? It'll just accelerate his evolution into a deadbeat. If he turns out to be the kind of guy who sponges off women, I'll be the one who suffers for it, and then his wife. In Komachi terms, I'd like my brother to come by his happiness honestly."

"I-is that right…? …Heh, deep stuff, coming from a middle schooler…"

This middle schooler really is deep. How did she end up this great? Does she have some deadbeat in her family? I must give thanks to them for being a great negative example.

X   X   X

Perhaps it was because the initial investment was small, or perhaps it was because we shared the earnings among all of us, but our medals ran out unexpectedly fast.

As if she had been waiting for the very moment when we were at loose ends and wondering what to do next, Komachi looked all of us over and made her move. "All right, we're out of medals, and we don't have much more time, so let's move on to one last game."

"One last game? What are you planning?" I asked.

We're still doing something? I'd thought for sure we were going home.

When everyone turned to her expectantly, Komachi declared in a resounding voice, "The Trans-Chiba Ultra Quiz~!"

As all our mouths dropped open, Komachi alone added a *duh-duh-duh-duuuhhhh!* and pointed over to the arcade cabinet behind her. "And so we will compete for victory with this game right here: *Quiz Magic Chibademy!*"

"Quiz Magic Chibademy *is starting~.*"

Now we've got some kind of knockoff of that quiz game I like to play... What demand for this game would there be outside Chiba? In fact, I doubt there's demand even within Chiba.

Komachi inserted a coin, the machine replied with a *bading, bading,* and the game was starting. It seemed she was doing this whether we liked it or not.

"All right, Miss Hiratsuka. Please read out the questions and be the judge," Komachi instructed.

Miss Hiratsuka agreed without a fuss. "Hmm, all right."

The cabinet steadily progressed through the opening screens to get *Quiz Magic Chibademy* started, but we ran into a problem.

"This is, like, supposed to be a single-player game. It's a me game," I pointed out.

Komachi chuckled smugly. "So we'll play in team battles. You'll be divided into groups, so please answer however you like. The rules are... Well, just figure out what works best as we go along, please."

"Your explanation just got very sloppy all of a sudden...," Yukinoshita said, putting a hand to her temple.

You said it. Just figure out what works as you go? What the hell is that supposed to be, everyday life in Japan?

Well, there were only two cabinets, so that meant we had no choice but to put together two teams and muddle through with a spirit of compromise.

"How should we divide up the teams?" Totsuka asked, glancing around.

Looking awkward enough to arouse suspicion, Yuigahama raised her hand. "Ah, if we're doing team battles, then I'll...go with H-Hikki... Um, for Chiba knowledge reasons..."

Well, that was a reasonable choice. I'd be at the greatest advantage among all of us when it came to knowledge of Chiba. It was practically inevitable that whatever team had me on it would win... As long as our teamwork wasn't tested, then it'd probably work out for us.

Whether she was aware of these motives or not, Komachi shook her head no. "Let's split into guys and girls."

Hmm, well, that *was* the simplest way, which meant my team would be me, Zaimokuza, and...Totsuka, huh? Totsuka's allowed to be on our team, right?

I was about to begin some very ponderous pondering, but when I saw Totsuka's brilliant smile, I didn't care anymore.

"So then you and me'll be on the same team, Hachiman?"

"Yeah. Let's do this, Totsuka."

Yeah, let's do this!

As I was overflowing with motivation, I could hear a cheerless voice off to the side. "Huh? Oh..." Yuigahama seemed dissatisfied.

Komachi sneaked up to her. "Yui, Komachi has an idea."

"O-oh, I know that smile~. That's the scary one she gets when she's getting ideas~..."

Komachi hopped away from Yuigahama, then turned back to me—and what I saw was a grin that made me very nervous. "Heh-heh-heh... Right, then! Let's get started! The losing team is gonna get punished!" With that, she gave her usual cutesy smile as she declared the start of the game.

X   X   X

As the tension of competition ran, Miss Hiratsuka stood before the two cabinets. This game of *Quiz Magic Chibademy*, this Chibaluation, had both our pride and a punishment hanging on it, and the teacher was just about ready to fire the starting gun.

With my love for Chiba, I could not allow myself to lose so easily.

Miss Hiratsuka looked over us all and took a deep breath. Then she cried out, "Do you want to go to the Ostrich Kingdom?!"

"Whoo!"

"Whoo!"

"Yea!"

Komachi, Totsuka, and Zaimokuza all shot up their hands. Meanwhile, Yukinoshita and Yuigahama could tell they'd missed something and tilted their heads.

"What's the Ostrich Kingdom...?" Yukinoshita asked.

"I kinda don't really wanna go..."

What, these guys don't know the Ostrich Kingdom? "It's a pretty fun place. Like, the ostrich sashimi is really good."

"You can eat ostriches...?" Yuigahama was rather taken aback.

Ostrich is known to be low calorie and high protein, though. Its light meaty texture is excellent. The eggs have a pretty complex flavor.

As my mind was busy exploring ostrich-related thoughts, the game had already gotten started. I heard Miss Hiratsuka reading out a question. "Question: 'Chiba prefecture's mascot is—'"

Before she could even finish reading out the question, my teammate Zaimokuza pressed the answer button. "Herm, leave this to I," he said, brimming with confidence, and then with a flutter of his trench coat, he pointed at Miss Hiratsuka. "...The wind crimson hound, Chiiba-kun!"

Why are you calling it that...?

Miss Hiratsuka shook her head, and soon after came the tragic buzzing sound effect. She'd still been in the middle of the question, so now she read out the rest. "'…is Chiiba-kun, but…'"

"Ngh, a trick question!" Zaimokuza slammed the button in frustration.

Uh, that isn't a trick question or anything; this is common sense with quiz games. The way questions are written, it becomes clear what they're asking after a certain point. That's what they said in *Fastest Finger First*.

"Come on, Zaimokuza…" I gave him a little glare.

But he just stuck out his tongue and rapped his knuckles on his own head. "Tee-hee. ☆"

"Tch, you really get on my nerves…"

As I was silently letting Zaimokuza know he was a dead man later, Miss Hiratsuka decided she was done with listening to us and attempted to move things along. "Continuing the question. 'Chiba prefecture's mascot is Chiiba-kun, but what color is he?'"

Now the question was clear. I pressed the button without hesitation.

But I was a second too slow, and Komachi won the right to answer. "Komachi gets it! The answer is red!"

When she got it correct, the decorative lights flashed in a gaudy dance, and Komachi twirled along with them. Well, that one was just so easy, it was *too* easy… I suppose we could call it a warm-up.

Komachi and Yuigahama high-fived with a *yay!* And then Yukinoshita muttered, "Why is Chiiba-kun red anyway?"

"I—I dunno… I dunno that…" Why *is* he red? I don't feel like Chiba makes you think of the color red. I doubt he's just so brimming with passion that it makes him shine red…

As I was pondering this, Miss Hiratsuka addressed me. "You don't mind if we move on to the next one, right? Question: 'What is the first man-made coastline built in Japan, located in Chiba?'!"

Ohhh, this one was a little tough. None of us could push the buttons.

Then, though his face was pensive, Totsuka reached out. "U-um… K-Kujuukuri Beach?"

And then came the buzzer indicating a wrong answer.

Dejected, Totsuka put his hands together apologetically. "I'm sorry, Hachiman."

"You've got guts, little firefighter. You'll never get it right if you don't give it a shot. It's totally fine, don't worry, s'all good!"

I figured I'd take advantage of the opportunity to wrap an arm or two around him, but someone popped right between us. "H-Hachiman! I—I, too! I've been trying so hard, too!"

Why has he been trying to make himself look cute lately? Is he expecting Saint Bernard levels of demand? He's more like a Tosa, though.

"Yeah, yeah. I get it, I get it. Leave the rest to me." I casually warded off Zaimokuza, then turned to face the arcade cabinet again. What could I do to rid Totsuka of his guilt for making that mistake? I could get this answer right—that was what.

I fixed my glare on the answer button and pressed it with absolute confidence.

When the *ding-dong* sound effect rang out, Miss Hiratsuka smirked. "Mm-hmm, Hikigaya. Your answer?"

"The answer is…Inage Beach." I could hear myself swallow. Or maybe it was someone else. There was the briefest silence.

And then the *ding-dong, ding-dong* bell rang loud and clear like victory applause, declaring my answer was correct.

"Heh, if it's about Chiba, this is basically what you get," I said with a triumphant air. But what the heck was with that super-obscure question? Nobody but me, with my quiz skills and overflowing love for Chiba, would have been able to answer that.

Miss Hiratsuka nodded and *hmm*'d, raising both index fingers. "Now both teams are even. All right, onward and upward!" She made a fist, and motivation coursed through me. I laid my hand on the answer button and prepared for action.

"Question: 'Chiba's local specialty dish—'"

"Katsuura dan-dan men!"

"Question: 'What sweets shop in Bousou Kyoudo—?'"

"Orandaya!"

"Question: 'Despite being in Chiba—'"

"Tokyo German Village!"

"Question: 'Which eminent Chiba figure—?'"

"Tadataka Inou!"

I answered question after question, without missing a beat. My chain of victories, my indomitable string of correct answers, created a stir of excited murmurs among the competitors.

"Wow, Hachiman!" Totsuka smiled at me and clapped, while Zaimokuza grinned proudly and slapped my shoulder.

"Herm. Hachiman, you are number one."

But I'm really nothing special. "No, I'm not number one. It's Chiba that's number one. Despite being number three in Kanto." After Tokyo and Kanagawa, Chiba is always firmly in third place. So, like, you know, you can call it third place nationally. And if you go off the name of the Makuhari New City area, you can even call Chiba a city, too.

The boys' team was boiling with the certainty of victory, but the girls' team was less excited. Komachi was so frustrated, she was practically grinding her teeth. "Ngh, as expected of my brother. He's got it bad for Chiba…"

"At this rate, we'll lose to Hikki and the guys…," Yuigahama muttered.

Yukinoshita had seemed disinterested up until this point, but that remark made her twitch. "Lose…losing to Hikigaya…," she muttered as if in a delirium, and then her eyes opened wide. With her fighting spirit quietly burning, she reached out to the answer button.

"Y-Yukinon is on fire…" Her intensity pulled a shudder from Yuigahama.

Miss Hiratsuka, who enjoyed it when things got competitive, smirked and read out another question. "'The local food commonly associated with Chiba's Choshi city—'"

I got this! It didn't matter if Yukinoshita was getting serious now; when it's about Chiba, it's my field, my garden—it's my whole house. She might beat me in exam scores, but there was no reason for her to beat me now. With absolute confidence, I pressed the button and instantly responded, "*Nure-senbei!*"

The moment I answered this, Miss Hiratsuka broke into a smile. "'…is *nure-senbei*, but…'"

"Ngh, damn it…" Under the force of Yukinoshita's intensity, I'd become thoughtlessly overeager. Zaimokuza looked over at me and gave me an irritatingly smug chuckle. *I get it. I'm sorry…*

Even as I avoided Zaimokuza's eyes, the question continued.

"'…But what's the number one recommended way of eating them?'!"

"There's no way I could know that!" Yuigahama cried out indignantly.

But someone else immediately slammed the button. "Leave it to Komachi!"

That's no good… Komachi often eats *nure-senbei* with me, so I knew she was gonna answer this one right…

"The answer is…you cook them in a toaster oven and eat them with mayonnaise and *shichimi!*" Komachi replied.

Yuigahama's face scrunched up, and Yukinoshita brought her eyebrows together.

"Sounds like a lot of calories…"

"*Nure-senbei* are wet… Should you be cooking them…?"

It's fine; they taste good cooked. But I guess I can't deny the high-calorie part.

And then the fanfare for the correct answer rang out.

"It was right, too…," Yuigahama said with some dismay.

It's good, though. You should try it out.

Cheered by her correct answer, Komachi puffed out her chest smugly. "Leave all pointless Chiba knowledge to me. Komachi's always been the only one to listen to Bro talk about Chiba, so I've just picked this stuff up!"

"Whoa, weird siblings…"

Hey there? Yuigahama? Don't you think that judgment is a little too blunt? Whatever, we're just close. I seriously considered protesting, but Miss Hiratsuka didn't give us any time for that and started reading out the next question.

"Question: 'What Chiba marine product is fished most in Chiba, out of all of Japan?'"

The moment the question was finished, a hand smashed the answer button with lightning speed. "Ise lobster," Yukinoshita said, in a flawless pose.

What was that? There was absolutely zero delay there...

"How do you know that, too, Yukinon?! You're kinda weird!" Yuigahama said.

But that wasn't anything to be startled by. Academically speaking, that would count as a geography question, and Yukinoshita is well versed in Chiba, too. Perhaps because of her father's job.

Even so, most people still wouldn't know that. Sounding impressed, Totsuka said, "We catch Ise lobster, even here in Chiba? And the most in the country, too..."

"Yeah, geez," I said. "Then they should just change the name to Chiba lobster." They're called Ise lobster, but Ise isn't number one in that category; what's up with that? Is it like how Tokyo German Village is named after Tokyo, even though it's in Chiba? Okay, that makes sense.

Anyway, hearing that answer just now, it hit me again how Yukinoshita excels in the strangest ways. "As expected of Yukipedia."

"Stop calling me that." Yukinoshita swept her hair off her shoulder and gave me an icy glare.

Even Komachi got in on the angry reaction. "That's right, Bro. You've got to call her Yukino."

"Hey, man...I can't call her that... My life would be in danger." Sheer terror turned my last sentence into a whisper. I sneaked a fearful glance over at Yukinoshita to see her response, but she quietly turned her face away.

"O-of course..................I can't have you...calling me that."

"Agh, are we done?" Miss Hiratsuka's sigh drowned out Yukinoshita's remark, and I didn't hear her finish.

Our teacher cleared her throat and paused for effect. "This final question is your hammer chance!"

"Chance!" For some reason, Zaimokuza reacted to that one word.

Miss Hiratsuka completely ignored him and began her explanation. "For our last question, if you use this golden hammer to get the right answer, you win ten thousand points."

"So what was the rest of the quiz for? This basically makes me an idiot for having answered all those questions. What is this, a microcosm of life?"

You can steadily work toward your goals, but you won't necessarily succeed. It's too common for connections, nepotism, the whims of those in power, the schemes of your superiors, or any number of things to topple everything and ensure your efforts were in vain.

I have learned yet another truth of the world…

But that was exactly why I couldn't let myself lose. I don't care what garbage rules I use myself to win with no effort, but I will firmly stand up against any sort of twisted regulations that allow anyone else to play the grasshopper mooching off the ant's hard work.

Zaimokuza must have sympathized with this spirit, as he thrust his fist up toward me. "Hachiman, I entrust this to you. Use the Goldeon Hammer!"

"O-okay… It's a golden hammer, though."

Is this okay? Are we gonna be okay? Well, as long as this little problem doesn't turn problematic, it's no problem. But never mind that now—I've got this quiz problem.

Finally, the last question. The one question that would decide this long battle. Wait, we're settling it with just this one question? Really?

"Question: 'We asked one hundred high school girls in Chiba prefecture this: What is your go-to date spot?'"

I carefully waited until it was clear what the question was, then cautiously pressed the button.

The timing of my button press was no problem. I'd made sure to get ahead of the opposition. If you assume that he who moves first is the victor, my victory was assured.

So I'd just use my allotted time to the last second as I derived the correct answer.

The question had been deliberately prefaced with *Chiba prefecture*, but the high school girl is a fairly consistent creature across regions. They're not Pokémon, so they won't have a habitat-based distribution.

Furthermore, they are sensitive to trends, and in general, they are always ready to find some sort of mainstream to join. Therefore, the limiting condition of *Chiba prefecture* would have no function in this question.

Additionally, the term *date spot* makes transparent the preference of the sort of girl who would go to the trouble of responding to this survey. If they were responding to this survey, then it wasn't difficult to imagine that they were glorifiers of romance.

Further, we could also establish that the condition of *high school girl* encompasses features of youth and immaturity, which also points to purity and aspiration to adulthood.

The answer derived based on the above conditions is…

I can see it! My final answer! Though it's a little embarrassing to say…

"…H-her boyfriend's house?"

The unpitying buzzer rang out, and everything went dead silent.

They all looked at one another's faces uncomfortably and then began talking in whispers.

"That was a surprisingly normal answer…," Yuigahama muttered, as if she couldn't endure this any longer.

Kindly, perhaps attempting to be considerate, Miss Hiratsuka asked me, "…Hikigaya, is that what you want it to be?"

"The strange realism of that fantasy is what makes it so sad." And then, like an executioner with her guillotine, Yukinoshita finished me off with a final remark. Depending on your interpretation, decapitation can be a man's salvation.

"Kuh! This is really embarrassing… Just kill me! I'd rather you just finish me off!"

As I was beginning to despair, Totsuka and Zaimokuza came in to support me.

"I-it's okay, Hachiman," said Totsuka. "It sounded like you put a lot of thought into that answer, so I'm sure it'd make a girl happy!"

"Verily so, Hachiman. I also often have such thoughts. It's naught to be ashamed of!"

"R-right? It's not weird for a boy, right?!"

Totsuka is so angelic, I want *him* coming over to my house

sometime soon. Zaimokuza's fantasies, though, are a little gross! *In fact, if I'm in the same category as Zaimokuza, I really am me after all*, I thought, and then the depression set in.

Then, a beaming smile on her face, Komachi patted my shoulder. "There, there. It's okay. You've got Komachi at home, and that just now was worth a lot of Komachi points."

"Don't try to console me with pitying looks, and don't try to earn points. You're making me feel even more pathetic."

Plus, if I have Komachi at home, that's basically a little sister true end where my girlfriend is Komachi and every day is a date. What the heck, is this some Chiba anime?

I was beat up so bad, I wasn't just at 0 HP, I was at Zero Requiem, but there was yet more they could take from me.

"Since that was incorrect, the golden hammer goes to the opposing team."

The golden hammer was mercilessly yoinked away and handed over to the opposing team. Well, if you blow your chance, you're gonna get kicked while you're down. That's just typical of life.

Then the girls got their chance for a comeback.

"Yuigahama, take it away." Yukinoshita must have seen that she was at a disadvantage on this question. She ceded it to Yuigahama, who had a higher probability of being able to answer, while Komachi balled a fist to cheer Yuigahama on.

"You can do it, Yui!"

"Y-yeah…" Yuigahama accepted their encouragement and, with a nervous look on her face, pressed the answer button. "Um…the answer is…Tokyo Destiny Land!"

And then, in celebration of her victory, the sound effect for the correct answer rang loud.

X X X

The noise returned to the arcade, and even louder than before, Komachi called out gleefully, "Announcing the results!" Just like she had the first time, she added her own *duh-duh-duh-duuuuh*, then retreated a step to cede the spot to Miss Hiratsuka.

The teacher nodded and grinned broadly. "Mm-hmm! With ten thousand and three points, the girls' team wins."

"I don't like this…" But, well, it was pointless to grumble. The world is always cruel—absurd, even. Effort is worth less than miracles. All the losers can do is congratulate the victors who emerge as a result of those miracles. It's thanks to the losers that victors are born, and this act substantiates that fact.

We applauded them, and as the girls celebrated, they also began a discussion. They must have been deciding what our punishment would be.

"You're the reason we won, Yui, so you can make the request."

"Yes, I believe that's appropriate. If I had been the one to win, I would have no complaints with that, and I didn't have my heart set on any particular request."

Komachi yielded the right to decide, and Yukinoshita agreed.

Yuigahama was bewildered by their reaction. Well, she didn't often decide things herself, so the sudden weight of this responsibility must have made her uncomfortable. "Huh? But I can't just…"

When Yuigahama considered and groaned over this and that, Komachi tiptoed up to her. "Yui, Yui. Let me talk to you a sec."

"Huh? What?" Yuigahama tilted her head toward Komachi, beside her.

"Psst, psst, psst."

"…Hmm, hmm… Huh? Ohhh~. Th-that's kind of embarrassing…" I don't know what Komachi said, but Yuigahama was red to the ears.

Figuring they were done with their discussion, Miss Hiratsuka turned back to us. "And now for the announcement of the punishment," she said and glanced over at Yuigahama, prompting her.

"Uh, um…Hikki." And there, Yuigahama briefly came to a halt. I said nothing, either, waiting for her to continue.

Yuigahama took a few big, deep breaths, and once she was calm, she glanced up at me through her lashes. "…Let's…hang out again?"

Reserved though it was, this was a tiny step—no, maybe half a step? Like she was testing the waters, close enough to be almost intrusive. If you were to put that distance into a number, I'm sure it would just be a couple of centimeters. And most likely, if you were to put it into words, you would call this distance "elbow room"—or maybe like the play of a steering wheel before it starts to engage.

This subtle distance, like a buffer zone for preventing wear and abrasion, was fitting for us now, and that was why I was able to respond after a bit of a pause.

"…Well, if that's my punishment, I don't have a choice."

Yes. There was no escaping my punishment.

This is the guilt the loser should shoulder, the punishment they must accept. So I was okay hanging out with them just one more time.

Upon hearing my answer, Yuigahama blew out a breath so deep even her shoulders deflated. She gave a sunny smile, as if this had dislodged something stuck in her chest. I looked away in embarrassment.

And there, I saw Komachi nodding in a manner that rubbed me the wrong way.

I could see exactly what my little sister was thinking, but since her heart was so easy to read, I couldn't decide if I should get angry or not. As I was scratching my head and wondering what to do, someone unexpected broke the silence.

"Oh yeah! Let's all hang out again!" That soft, buoyant tone was like an angel's feathers.

The sudden remark confused Komachi. "…Hmm?"

When she turned to look, there was Totsuka, trotting up with a beaming smile of anticipation. Without a thought, I replied to him with an enthusiastic, silent cry, something resembling an *uh-huh!* or a *yeah!* or a *yep, yep!*

"Huh? T-Totsuka? In Komachi terms, that wasn't supposed to be, like, everyone…"

Flustered, Komachi tried to slide between me and Totsuka, but a large black shadow popped up to prevent her. "Herm, well then, I shall also stand by your side! B-but I just mean it like, hanging out! D-don't get the wrong idea, Hachiman!"

"I won't. There's nothing to get the wrong idea about." *Seriously, what's Zaimokuza trying to lure me in with here...?* I thought. My exasperation must have been contagious, as Yuigahama chuckled, too.

"This…isn't exactly what I was thinking, but it seems fun, so oh well," she said, spinning around to smile at Yukinoshita.

Realizing what she meant by that smile, Yukinoshita breathed a short sigh and replied with a small nod. "Yes. I'm not very good at group activities, but if you don't mind, then I'll accompany you when I have the time."

Yuigahama welcomed Yukinoshita's kindness and glomped the other girl. "Yeah, it's a promise. I love you, Yukinon!"

"Hey, could you not cling to me like that? I *said* if I have the time." Yukinoshita twisted around in an attempt to escape, but there was no indication she would ever be released.

Miss Hiratsuka watched the two of them with a faraway look in her eyes. "It's so nice to be young…"

Hurry! Someone hurry up and marry this woman!

There was one more person with us, a complicated expression on her face as she watched from afar. "Oof, that was an unexpected obstacle… Komachi's magnificent plan… Bro's youth romantic comedy is all wrong, as I expected…"

Ha-ha-ha, better luck next time, Komachi. How disappointing.

No matter what plans you try to put together, your big brother will end up getting asked out by a boy and reacting with delight.

…Actually, I get the feeling the big brother is the disappointment here.

Short Story 3
Unexpectedly, **Hachiman Hikigaya**'s studying methods are not wrong.

It was around the time when fall was nearing its peak after the cultural festival, and the Service Club room had suddenly become chilly enough to rival the temperature outside. The cause was the aforementioned Chiba Prefecture–Wide Advice E-mail.

We'd received yet another hopeless e-mail again that day, and after reading it out, Yuigahama gave a quiet "Whoa…"

```
Request for advice from username: Master Swordsman
General
    Master Hachiman… I want to write a light novel that
will sell (trembling voice).
```

Yukinoshita, who'd been listening to Yuigahama read this out, addressed me without closing her paperback. "Sounds like this one's for you, Hikigaya."

Thank you very much for requesting me! I'm Hachiman! ♪ (sideways peace sign ☆)

I had to force myself to be excited in my head or else my spirit would break. Couldn't we add this domain to the block list or something? My anger and irritation toward the corruption of IT companies manifested in some rather violent typing as I hammered out the message.

Response from the Service Club:
Personally, I think the important features of best-
selling light novels are 1) the illustrations, 2) the
imprint, there's no 3 or 4, and 5) arm-twisting. Based
on the above, please do your best.

Yukinoshita narrowed her eyes doubtfully as she scanned what I was about to send. Then she tilted her head. "Which one is supposed to be the author's effort...?"

"Either three or four," I replied.

Then Yuigahama, who'd been reading the e-mail with a similar dubious look, raised her head. "...You don't need those?"

"If you just want to sell, I don't think so. He's not asking to write an interesting light novel, but one that'll sell. Those aren't necessarily the same thing," I said. Yuigahama gave an impressed *ohhh*, while Yukinoshita gave a little convinced nod.

Yes, selling and being interesting are not the same thing. That's why I like Gagaga Bunko! Where sales are always falling and nothing is popular—those are the books I'm waiting for!

So now that that was dealt with—or rather, now that the buck had been passed to me so that she didn't have to deal with it—Yukinoshita must have been feeling more relaxed. For once, she was the one who started reading out the next e-mail. "All right, next. From Chiba city, username: I shouldn't have to write my name down to ask for advice."

Request for advice from username: I shouldn't have
to write my name down to ask for advice
My little brother is taking the high school entrance exams this year, so I want to know if you have
any efficient studying techniques.

That curt style and harsh username, plus the topic was a little brother—I couldn't help but think of a familiar face.

"You're good at this sort of thing, aren't you, Yukinoshita?" I asked.

Yukinoshita put her hand to her jaw and began considering.

"Efficiency... It's not something I've ever actively thought about. I just study normally... Actually, wouldn't underhanded methods be your area of expertise for times like these?"

"At least call me resourceful... And I do it like normal, too. I solve lots of questions from past exams and go over all the ones I got wrong. Depending on the subject, I might memorize the whole problem."

"That's surprisingly legitimate..." Yukinoshita was sincerely surprised.

Hey, that's a little rude... I mean, it's not like I never think about being sneaky, but it's a real headache to actually do. "Techniques for entrance exams do exist, but learning them requires practice and repetition, too."

"They do say there's no shortcut to scholarship," Yukinoshita said, the height of seriousness.

"Then do we just reply with that?"

As I considered writing up a reply of that nature, Yuigahama stood up with a thump, unable to take it anymore. "Hey, why aren't you asking me?! I took the entrance exams, too! I passed, you know?!"

Yukinoshita paid no heed to Yuigahama's attempt to draw attention to this fact, instead looking at the computer screen with a little *ah.* "There's more to the e-mail. ...Also, I'd like to know how I can help him refresh after studying, it says."

"Finally, your time to shine, Yuigahama! Tell us a way he can perk up!"

"Hikki! That smirk is making me mad! I mean, I'm thinking hard about this, too!" Quite peeved, Yuigahama snatched away the laptop and moaned to herself as she slowly typed out an e-mail.

Response from the Service Club:
How about you study together with him? If you're always telling him to study, study, study, he might stop wanting to do it. The most efficient thing is to do it when you feel motivated (for me, at least). So, if you study alongside him, Kawasaki, he should feel like, "I have to do it, too!" Oh, and you might

get better results if you teach him things he doesn't understand! And then once you're done studying, if you chat about like fun stuff that happened at school, I think that will perk him right up! You can do it!

Yuigahama chuckled, seeming rather proud to have finished writing that. Well, I could see it. I was a little surprised after reading it, and it seemed Yukinoshita was, too.

"...That's actually a legit good response," I said.

"Yes, it's unusual for Yuigahama to write something decent..."

"That's the unusual thing here?!" Yuigahama wailed, nearly in tears as she beat her fists against Yukinoshita's chest.

Watching them from the corner of my eye, I wondered if the rarity of decent answers from us meant this club was kinda sorta no good.

Also, I'd like to know how I can

help him refresh after studying.

SS
3

Special Act: Side-B
They have yet to know of a place they should go back to.

The term's exams ended, and the rainy season came to a close.

Though the long spell of rain was over, the heavy showers still came frequently, and always when I was walking home. This was all probably because the air was filled with a humidity that constantly clung to your skin.

Being that it's on the coast, Soubu High School especially gets tons of moisture from the ocean. The damp sea wind fades bicycles and paint, and then it rusts the exposed iron of the fences.

But though the air was muggy, my mood was strangely clear.

This time of year, with summer vacation right around the corner, was exciting not only for the normies with their fun-packed plans, but also for the loners, who would be freed from the prison of school.

Might I call this the magic of summer?

Sometimes the heat makes people lose their minds.

This was why I was behaving so strangely and going against my better judgment. This was abnormal for me, and I couldn't make heads or tails of it myself.

The space between the rear of the school and the new building is shaded from the sun, which makes it especially cool there. From a bird's-eye view, the school building resembles a square, and the new building an extra line along one of the edges. Most students don't know this spot; some will pass by when they come from the martial arts dojo beneath the gym and the athletic clubrooms, but even then, nobody is around during lunch.

Which meant the only ones here were me and one other person.

With lunch break and summer break before them, the students bubbled with excitement. The wind carried the faint smell of the sea toward us.

And behind the school building, we spent this secret time alone together, just the two of us.

Now, this phrasing might imply I was having a youthful summer experience.

I was not.

"Heh-heh-heh, good of you to come. My fated enemy—Hachiman!" he said dramatically, stupidly, and obnoxiously.

My reply was apathetic. "I have finally cornered you, Master Swordsman General." It was such a monotone, even a TV personality or movie director working as voice actor would probably do a better job. Zaimokuza, opposite me, smoothly posed. Barf Spark–level obnoxious.

This was the reality.

Zaimokuza and I had simply fled somewhere deserted to hide alone together behind the school, so as not to be seen. By the way, I think that salty smell was sweat. Descriptive tricks are scary!

I'd been peacefully eating my lunch alone in my usual spot, watching Totsuka from a distance as he did his noontime practice, when Zaimokuza had cornered me. I'd been forced to read the plot of Zaimokuza's novel, and then before I knew it, I was being made to join in on his M-2-syndrome charade in the middle of the heat.

This is my reality, the summer of my second year in high school. Japan's summer is not Kincho's summer.

"Herm... Why such a lack of enthusiasm, Hachiman?! Why do you not face me in a fighting stance! This will not evoke my vision!" Zaimokuza complained to me, stomping on the ground.

Uh, come on... I'd said I didn't get the outline he'd written up, so Zaimokuza had started acting it out, and suddenly, here we were.

But logic wasn't going to work on Zaimokuza. That's just how he is. The correct tactic was to oppose him not with logic but with emotion. I swiftly put on a contemptuous smile. "…Oh, you mean this stance? This is the…actionless stance. By relaxing your whole body, you make to turn aside all forms of attack."

"Whoa, what a cool idea!"

Considering that I'd just come up with some bullshit I'd learned from *Rurouni Kenshin*, Zaimokuza really took the bait. He started clacking along on his smartphone like, *I'll take that!* I'd waffled as to whether I should say that or the Tenchi-matou stance, but if he wanted to use it, then great.

"Ngh, from a dodge and nullification to a sermon punch… Everyone will be talking about this…"

I ignored Zaimokuza's muttering and leaned against the wall. It seemed his problem had been solved, so I was free.

I'd gotten unpleasantly sweaty during my involuntary involvement in this nonsense. The blowing breeze felt good on my hot cheeks. When I twisted around a little to get the wind to blow my hair back like T.M.Revolution, an unusual sight caught my eye.

A few boys in judo uniforms were trudging toward us with drooping shoulders. Awfully meek for a bunch of guys in intimidating martial arts uniforms.

I figured if they were going to the trouble of practicing during lunch hour, they were probably just as dedicated as my angel Totsuka, but was our school's judo club like that? Ah, My Angel Totsuka. I want to answer quiz questions right to make him grow.

Totsuka does his lunch practice refreshingly and cutely and fun-ly and cutely, but the judo club guys who passed us seemed different.

Well, there was no helping that. 'Cause Totsuka's special. He's special Totsuka—shortened as Totspecial. It's like Totsucute, but more special.

Meanwhile, the judo club guys, who were neither special nor cute nor Totsuka, wore lifeless expressions as they ambled like particularly exhausted zombies. *…Are you office workers?!*

Leaning against the wall, I slid down to sit on the ground.

Zaimokuza must have noticed me glancing over at the aforementioned judo club group, as he tilted his head and made one of his noises. "What a suspicious group."

"I think they're a lot better than you, though…" Wearing that long coat in summer, you could only be a pervert or Dr. Black Jack.

"Rferm. Well, when you get to my level, being that I'm a Master Swordsman…" Zaimokuza seemed to take that as a compliment, and he snorted in satisfaction. I know there's this English phrase *positive thinking*; does it actually mean *total clueless asshat*, or am I just misremembering?

But there would be no benefit in pointing out Zaimokuza's habit of misinterpreting things now. I'm sure in his head, that's how it is… In his head.

I shifted my gaze away from Zaimokuza to watch the judo guys turn a corner, and that was when I suddenly remembered. "That reminds me—you picked kendo for the martial arts option, huh?"

At this time of year, us second-years were doing martial arts in gym class, and we had to choose either judo or kendo. And you have to buy equipment for both judo and kendo, but getting a whole set of kendo stuff is expensive, so I'd gone with judo. Of course, I'd told my parents that I wasn't sure which I would go for, so to give me money for kendo. I am the pocket-money alchemist: the *Fullmetal Alchemist*.

I'd chosen judo, but Zaimokuza hadn't been there with me, so by process of elimination, that meant he'd chosen kendo. It was also possible Zaimokuza's existence itself had been eliminated.

"Homm, indeed, I chose kendo. Of course. What about it?"

"Well…I was just feeling sorry for whoever has to partner with you." He's really annoying even in regular gym classes, so once he's in his element with kendo, I'm sure he's even more obnoxious.

"Your concern is unnecessary, for I cannot use my true strength against regular students. I suppress my powers."

"Oh, I see…"

Translating that into modern language, it means, *I-it's embarrassing to let other people see my ideas, after all... So I keep it down. Y-you're the only one I show this stuff to, Hachiman!* What the heck, that's creepy.

Well, if Zaimokuza isn't bothering other people, then that's good. The reason loners are permitted to exist is because we cause no harm to others. A pheasant would not be shot but for its cries. However, if a pheasant makes no noise at all, it becomes less than a pheasant, discarded and unworthy of even being shot. It will either be treated as nonexistent or downright loathsome. Whichever the case, if it were *Another*, you'd be dead.

"What about you, Hachiman?" Zaimokuza asked with a pout. My attitude must have rubbed him the wrong way.

But my answer was quite simple, and nothing really surprising. "A guy from the judo club has been partnering with me. The rest of the time, I've just been practicing falling."

"Herm...that's not partnering; that's babysitting...," Zaimokuza said as he wiped away the sweat beading on his forehead with a sleeve.

But that's not something to be so surprised about. If you're doing a certain sport in gym class, inevitably, the kids in that club will draw the short straw. They'll be told to do demonstrations and forced to set up the equipment and clean up after. Off-the-clock labor is seen as perfectly acceptable—the dark side of athletics. All the rumors these days are about sports clubs members at risk for becoming corporate slaves—the rumors in my head, that is.

And so if those judo club guys were babysitting me, there was no helping that... Was that why they were looking so glum? Sorry.

But my showing worry wasn't going to change this custom. And of course, I couldn't skip class just out of some weird concern for them. Loners have no one to help them, so they're forced to diligently attend all their classes.

Sorry to the judo club guys, but I'm going to be bothering you for a while.

I dug in my heels, and right then, the bell rang to signal the end of lunch break. I stood and wiped the sand off my butt. "'Kay, I'm going back to the classroom," I said and turned away. Footsteps followed after me, as if this was the obvious thing to do.

"Hmon, well then, let us go."

Huh? He's coming back with me? I had implied I would be going back alone, hadn't I?

I shot Zaimokuza a questioning look, but he wasn't bothered by it. He even gave me an overbearing chuckle. "What are you doing? Be swift, hurry! Fly like the wind! Hyah, too slow! I'm going ahead!" He pointed aggressively to the school building. Translating what he just said into modern language, that meant, *What's wrong? Let's hurry up and go back... Oh, but if we were to go back together, people might talk... And that'd be embarrassing...* If I thought about it that way, I wouldn't get mad. Just a little grossed out.

× × ×

I finished off my afternoon classes and headed to the clubroom. Times were a-changing, as our school was equipped with internal heating and air conditioning, so that even in the summer, we could be comfortable in class. However, outside of the classrooms, it's a different story. Same with after school.

I walked down the hallway of the special building, my indoor shoes slapping along the floor.

Even on a hot day like this, every time I head to the Service Club room in the special building, I feel a little cooler. It must be because the room tends to be shady and open to the wind. Or is it because the master of this clubroom gives off a certain air? I think it's probably the latter and that this chill is more the kind that runs down your spine. Oh, and it's downright frigid near your heart, too!

As I was musing about the irrelevant coolness of the special building, I opened the door of the clubroom to be stabbed by the rather cold glance flicking my way.

"...Hey." I flinched under Yukino Yukinoshita's piercing gaze. *What, why's she angry?* Could she tell what I was thinking just now? If she could, then we'd have a major dispute between two theories: the "Yukinoshita is an esper theory," or the "I'm a *satorare* theory."

"...Oh, it was you, Hikigaya-kun? You looked so slimy, I thought an amphibian was walking in the door."

"No, I've just been soaking in the joys of youth. Nothing you can do about that. And don't say those things around Miss Hiratsuka. I don't think she'd like it." We greeted each other as we always did, and I took my position in my usual seat diagonally across from Yukinoshita.

Though Yukinoshita was in a mood, which was nothing new, she didn't really say anything more than that before dropping her eyes to the paperback in her hands.

I could tell she wasn't in the greatest mood, but it seemed the cause was not any resentment, hatred, or loathing toward me. Normally, she would have added a few more sarcastic quips, but that day, she was quiet. Well, it's more like she normally gives me way too much crap.

So if she wasn't annoyed with me, then why was she in such a bad mood? *Don't act like that; it ruins the vibe.* Come on, is she like one of those office worker ladies you have to tiptoe around because she acts wildly different depending on if she's in a good or bad mood?

I didn't have anything in particular to do, so I pulled my own paperback out of my bag, too. I flipped around a bit, skimming through it, occasionally glancing over at Yukinoshita.

"...Phew." All she was doing was reading, and yet, she gave a little sigh. Apparently, that was enough to stress her out. *Come on, is the book that boring? Then just stop reading it...*

Well, when you're dealing with a stress home generator, a stress home poisoner, nothing you can say will do any good. Only the one who's created the stress can deal with it.

I was dropping my gaze to my book once more, figuring I'd leave her be and focus on reading, when I heard the door slide open loudly.

"Yahallo!" Greeting us with a passion as suffocating as midsummer, Yuigahama jumped into the clubroom. Her footsteps pattered loudly as she went to sit in her usual spot.

Yuigahama had been wearing her skirt slightly shorter lately. Incidentally, she'd also stopped wearing navy-blue socks and started wearing mostly ankle socks. She'd also rolled up the arms of her short-sleeved blouse. She was in full summer mode. Compared with before, it was fair to say she was only exposing more of her arms and legs. Uh, it's not like I've been observing closely, though. It's just that you pick up on these things if you see her every day, that's all. Don't you underestimate the observational eye of a loner.

"It's so hot!" As soon as she was in her seat, Yuigahama grabbed the chest of her blouse and fanned herself with it.

Can you not? I can't help looking.

Now that I think of it, despite her complaints about the heat, she never unbuttons her shirt or wears polo shirts or anything. It's a little surprising. Like, does she just really want to keep wearing the ribbon in front?

I turned my attention to the paperback in my hands to avoid looking at Yuigahama as much as possible. Whereupon the paper, which was damp with the humidity already, was met with surplus force and got wrinkled.

Agh, I'll have to put a weight on this later to flatten it out... Incidents of this nature are a little sad for book lovers. That's another unpleasant thing about the season.

It wasn't as if Yuigahama was doing anything wrong. In fact, I was indeed completely at fault here—so, um, yeah, I'm sorry for looking—but since Yuigahama was the indirect cause of this situation, I couldn't help but glance at her a little reproachfully despite knowing it was unfair. No, this was not at all because I was marveling at how long her legs were in addition to admiring her chest-fanning. Ultimately, this was merely a look of unjustified resentment. Though both were terrible reasons to look.

But maybe the anxiety was needless, as Yuigahama failed to notice my gaze. Instead, her attention was on Yukinoshita. "What's wrong, Yukinon?"

Yukinoshita seemed in such a bad mood, I doubt anyone else would have tried to talk to her. In fact, initiating conversation is a pretty high bar to clear on a good day.

But Yuigahama could do that now.

Before, she would never have been so intrusive; she would have asked something inoffensive instead. Her ability to speak to Yukinoshita directly now was proof that they were closer.

Ever since Yuigahama's birthday, I'd gotten the feeling that they'd dropped some of the unnecessary tiptoeing and reservation between each other.

When Yuigahama spoke to her, Yukinoshita froze for a moment as if unsure whether to talk or not. But then she answered Yuigahama sincerely. "I wish we had a blow-dryer in here or something…"

"Ahhh, the humidity, huh? It really is annoying. So much for nice and smooth, right?"

Gently stroking her paperback, Yukinoshita breathed a sigh, while Yuigahama roughly ran her fingers through her own hair.

"I was referring to how moisture can result in serious damage… It's really stressful."

"Huh? You don't have damage," Yuigahama said, standing up and circling around behind Yukinoshita. Ignoring Yukinoshita's questioning look, she slid her hands down Yukinoshita's hair. "It's so smooth. Oh, but I guess it must make you feel a little hot."

"…Yuigahama? What are you doing?"

"Hmm. Here we go." Yuigahama rummaged around in her pocket and found something. She hooked it with a finger and spun it around. It looked like a hair elastic. She reached into her bag, too, pulled out a brush, then slowly and carefully brushed Yukinoshita's hair. She bundled together the long, glossy hair, twisted it together, and raised it up. "Long hair is hot in summer, so wouldn't it be more comfy like this?"

"O-oh, well, I suppose…" Yukinoshita replied to Yuigahama's question with hesitation. She must not have been used to having people fiddle with her hair, as she flinched a little. It was a rare sight. "Um, so…Yuigahama? Why are you touching my hair…? Um, are you listening?"

Of course Yuigahama was not listening.

She was humming as she bunched together Yukinoshita's hair and fixed the updo to finish it off. But even so, Yukinoshita's long black hair was spilling out awkwardly. Yuigahama clipped it in place with a hairpin she'd pulled from her chest pocket, and there was a bun.

"Done! ...I guess we kinda match." Yuigahama smiled with satisfaction and chuckled, gazing upon the completed hairdo. Indeed, if you were to compare the hairstyle—and only the hairstyle—they were similar.

"It's less like they match and more like one's a rip-off."

"Hey! You don't have to put it that way!" Yuigahama snapped at me. It seemed she was quite satisfied with her handiwork.

Uh, say what you want; that's the only way I can describe that... It's like the Tamagotchi and the Tamago Watch, or Digimon and Gyaoppi. I don't know what else to call something like this. "...Would you prefer *unlicensed variant?*"

"That's the same thing!"

I had been trying to be considerate, and I'd chosen words to make my intent slightly clearer... But I actually did have a hard time describing it. They weren't similar enough to call it a recolor, and really, the way they resembled each other despite not actually looking alike just made her look more like a knockoff...

"But, like, you're not bothered about having the same hairstyle or whatever?" I asked.

When you're at high school age, every other word out of your mouth is *unique, unique, unique.* I feel like girls tend to be like that, especially when it comes to fashion, so how does that factor in? Or is it that when you live like Yuigahama in a constant state of social awareness, that activates your Misuzu Kaneko armament: *Everyone is the same, and everyone is good?*

Yuigahama lifted her head and pondered this with a *hmm,* but considering how much time she took, her response was simple. "It doesn't bother you if you're friends, right?"

Oh, I see... You're friends, huh...?

I couldn't argue with such a sweet and serene answer. I breathed a short, rather exasperated little sigh, then returned to my reading.

Whereupon Yukinoshita, who'd been at Yuigahama's mercy and desperately trying to keep up, opened her mouth. "Um...what on earth have you done with my hair?" She couldn't tell what had gone on behind her head.

Yuigahama pulled a thin, square pink mirror out of her bag and handed it over. "Here!"

"Thanks." Yukinoshita placed her paperback on the desk, accepted the pocket mirror, and popped open the cover to look at herself. Her eyes narrowed, and her expression turned doubtful. Then she slapped the mirror shut and turned that doubtful gaze on Yuigahama. "...Yuigahama, why did you do this?" she asked.

Yuigahama blinked a few times. "Huh? Weren't we talking about how your hair was being stupid and making you grumpy?"

"I was talking about *this*." Yukinoshita pointed at her book on the desk and continued. "The humidity damages books, and I'll have to dry it out eventually, which will take time...so I was a little irritated."

"Oh, is that right...? I thought for sure..." Yuigahama gave a *ta-ha-ha* and scratched her head.

What with the talk of blow-dryers, they'd ended up having two separate conversations, huh? I get it. Personally, I like to keep the summer humidity at bay with my dry sense of humor.

Well, Yuigahama doesn't read books, so if she hears the word *blow-dryer*, her hair is probably the first thing that comes to mind. Their interests are in different fields.

On the other hand, while I don't think Yukinoshita is indifferent to fashion, she likes books more. And the summer humidity can indeed be pretty rough for a reader. Also, hand sweat makes the paper wrinkle. When droplets of sweat hit the paper, the way it goes all limp can be a real mood-killer.

Yuigahama, smiling to cover her embarrassment, stood up as if she had just clued in. "Oh, s-sorry! I'll fix your hair!"

"I don't really mind." Yukinoshita jerked her gaze away. Despite her protests, she must have been thinking about it. She opened the pocket mirror again and casually turned her face to either side to check it out, cautiously combing at the bun part. "...It is cooler," she added eventually, but her cheeks were so much redder than before I doubted she'd cooled down at all. It seemed she liked her matching hair...

Seeing this, Yuigahama grinned happily and glomped Yukinoshita. "Right, right?!"

"There's no need for such fervor...," Yukinoshita complained. She was acting grumpy, but it just looked like she was trying to hide her shyness.

And yet, instead my heart was left cold as ice...

Well, Yukinoshita's cheered up, and I can leave the rest to these two young'uns. Guess that means I can go home! Right, going home. I tucked my paperback away in my bag and stood as quietly as possible to avoid detection. I took a step toward the door, but right then, we heard a *knock, knock.*

"Come in," Yukinoshita called out, immediately inferring someone wanted in.

"'Scuse's 'sup!" With an incomprehensible greeting that sounded more like a gust of wind, a few grim-looking guys walked in. There were three of them: one like a potato, one like a sweet potato, and one like a taro.

It was a hot time of year to begin with, but the excess of hot-blooded manliness on display made it positively boiling. Immediately, my body temperature rose precisely three degrees.

X　X　X

The three boys standing at attention all had the same vibe, despite the variety in their appearances.

One of them was familiar to me, the potato boy. And he must have recognized my face, too, as he spoke to me. "Oh. It's you, from gym..."

"Yeah...," I replied briefly, with a raise of my hand. *Oh yeah, he's that nice guy who's been babysitting me in judo, in gym class.* He wasn't hovering around me constantly or anything, but he was a good guy. Though I didn't remember his name.

So does this mean the other two are from the judo club, too? I thought, glancing to the others, and Yuigahama and Yukinoshita looked at me.

"Friend of yours?"

"Acquaintance?"

There's a slight difference in the way you guys just asked me that question. Why's Yukinoshita assuming I have no friends...? I mean, she's not wrong. "Oh, I don't know his name. We're together in gym."

"You're together, but you don't know...?" Yuigahama was exasperated with me.

Well, some guys will get attached if you get weird and remember their names... More like I just don't go out of my way to remember names. When I was in middle school, they called me creepy just because I remembered everyone's names in class. That was the first time my good memory had ever backfired on me. Ever since then, I've made sure to put in only the most perfunctory effort to remember names. Like with Kawa-something.

I had intended to be considerate and converse quietly, but the potato's wry smile indicated he'd heard me. However, it seemed he hadn't remembered my name, either, so we were even.

The potato's voice was unexpectedly resonant and deep. "I'm Shiroyama. Judo club. These two are lowerclassmen..."

"Tsukui."

"Fujino."

Thank you very much for that macho trio self-intro. But the guys were somewhat lacking in defining characteristics, making them hard to remember. And being that they were hard to remember, I decided to dub them the Three Brothers Tuber: Potato, Sweet Potato, and Taro.

"I'm Yukinoshita, captain of the Service Club. This is Yuigahama, a member of the club." Yukinoshita gestured toward Yuigahama and introduced her.

Hmm, I think there's one more member, though?

But Yukinoshita didn't touch on that and instead moved on. "Now, then," she said to the Brothers Tuber, "are you informed as to what kind of activities this club engages in?"

"Yeah. Miss Hiratsuka told me you resolve issues at school...," said the potato, Shiroyama, henceforth known as Pota-yama.

Miss Hiratsuka again, huh...? Man, her explanations are half-assed. She's kinda making it out to be like Trouble Contractors, or TROCON, for short. Is there gonna be a coconut crab massacre?

Yukinoshita pressed her temple. "Strictly speaking, not quite..."

"Well, it's close enough," Yuigahama replied with a blank look.

I'm sure that's what it is, as Yuigahama understands it. It's just that Yukinoshita has those strange ideals of hers. From an outsider's perspective, we would be something like advice experts or an odd-jobs service.

Meaning if they'd come to us, the Brothers Tuber must have had some kind of problem. "So do you want something?" I asked.

The sweet potato and the taro both opened their mouths, but Pota-yama stopped them. Apparently, as their elder, he'd be the one to explain. What a good role model.

"Oh, um, it's difficult to talk about this, but…recently, a lot of our members have been talking about quitting. Some have already handed in their resignation forms." From his phrasing, I could guess Pota-yama was the club captain.

I'm jealous that they're even able to quit… I'd like to quit, too, but they won't let me, you know. This place violates employment standards, doesn't it?

My unethical employer *hmm*'d and put her hand to her chin in a thinking gesture. "People keep wanting to leave… Do you know why?"

"Well…" Shiroyama hesitated.

But frankly, I figured you didn't even have to ask. "That's just what the judo club is like, isn't it? It's like the three Ss: smell, strain, and severe exercise—what do you expect?" I said.

Sweet Potato and Taro fiercely argued with me.

"W-we don't smell!"

"But you're right about strain and severe exercise!"

I had no idea which was Tsukui and which was Fujino, but I could tell the sweet potato guy was sensitive about his BO, while the taro guy had no spine.

"Be quiet a minute," Pota-yama scolded them, and they backed down.

"Yessir."

Well trained. As expected of athletic types.

"You be quiet a minute, too, Hikigaya." Yukinoshita glared at me with cold eyes, and I obediently withdrew.

"Yessir…" I am also well trained.

Noticing the conversation had been interrupted, Shiroyama made us get back on topic. "You asked me if I know why?"

When he paused, Yuigahama gestured for him to proceed. "Mm-hmm, yeah."

"An older student, who graduated last year and is now in university, has been coming to watch practice. And he's a little…" It must have been pretty hard to say, as he trailed off into silence. But the remarks that followed made the situation abundantly clear.

"He's horrible!"

"He tortures us!" Unlike before, there was this tragic but brave note to their voices, and even Shiroyama didn't try to stop them, this time.

And the pair got even more passionate. "He'll be like, *It's a harsh world out there!* and totally run us through the wringer! He'll throw you so hard!"

"And whoever loses first in sparring has to go shopping for him! He'll make one guy eat ten beef bowls!"

"But when you try to use your moves on him, it just makes him mad!"

"He's crazy!"

Tsukui and Fujino cried out in alternation. Not only were they loud, but they were in such a rush to talk they ran out of breath and started panting. They would have said more, but Yukinoshita shot them a chilly glance, and they lost momentum and gradually fell silent.

After they were quiet, Yukinoshita said, "I understand the situation. So you're saying you want us to do something about this guy?"

As Yukinoshita said, this guy was the root of all these problems. At the very least, Sweet Potato and Taro seemed to hate him. The ones who wanted to leave the club probably felt the same.

So then the quickest thing to do would be to excise the afflicted part.

But Shiroyama shook his head and then gravely said, "…No, that's impossible."

"It is? Why?" Yuigahama tilted her head.

"If he listened to other people, it never would have gotten to this point… And besides, you're not even in the club. There wouldn't be much point if it came from you."

It seemed Shiroyama had spoken to this guy a number of times—probably gently, though. Shiroyama had been speaking vaguely, and I got the impression that when he talked about this guy, he chose his words carefully. I suppose he was showing discretion, or perhaps just keeping this guy at arm's length.

It's difficult for an outsider to butt in—and not just with clubs but with anything. If someone opens their mouth, it's human nature to think, *You don't know anything about us; shut up.* Even if they're right, you won't listen, no matter what.

So it would be best for someone with a connection to them to talk with them. "What about your advisor?" I asked.

Shiroyama's shoulders drooped. "He's not experienced in judo. When our senior visits, the advisor actually welcomes him, because he can take charge."

"Oh, then what about the third-years?" Yuigahama asked.

"They retired after the last tournament." Shiroyama answered that instantly, too. He had probably thought up these options himself already and given up on them as impossible solutions.

He'd already come to his conclusion.

"I don't think he'll listen, no matter who talks to him. He's good. He can't win against a team, but he's always won one-on-one. His skills are good enough to get him into university." Suddenly, Shiroyama's gaze turned distant, as if he were looking back on the past.

"Huh… Got in through a sports recommendation, huh? That's pretty amazing," I said.

So then based on my calculations, he would have been in third year when we were in first year. And since Shiroyama knew this guy, too, it made it hard for him to argue. To say nothing of his talent. So then even the current third-years wouldn't be able to oppose him, and it would be hard for an amateur advisor to interfere.

Yeah, so that would mean they just had to be quiet and put up with it. Skill and age-based hierarchical structures can't be broken down that easily.

After listening in silence for so long, Yukinoshita drew her hand away from her jaw. "If your request isn't to deal with this graduate, can I take it that you're looking to sign up new members?" she asked.

Shiroyama gave a slight nod and answered, "Yeah. I don't think this'll kill our club, but at this rate, we won't be able to put together a team for tournaments."

"Sign-ups, huh…?" I muttered. "It's not like you're getting people onto cell phone contracts, so I don't think it'll be that easy, though…"

Especially since this was the judo club. Someone would have to like judo—or just have an interest in it to begin with—or they wouldn't really consider joining. Maybe it's unkind to say this, but I wouldn't say it's a popular club for high school kids.

"Wouldn't it be better to get the people who quit to come back?" Yuigahama said, and Yukinoshita crossed her arms and nodded.

"Indeed. At the very least, they would have an interest in judo, which would make them more likely to join compared with the general student body."

Yuigahama seemed glad Yukinoshita agreed with her opinion, flinging her arms around the other girl. "Yeah, yeah! Plus, like, you can feel like you overcame it together and become closer friends!"

Yukinoshita seemed a little annoyed, but she didn't reject Yuigahama harshly. She gently pushed Yuigahama's hands away in an attempt to somehow maintain distance. Their similar hairstyles made the exchange look quite amicable.

I do think they have gotten closer. After Yuigahama's brief departure and return recently, I think you could indeed say there's been progress in their relationship. But their example is kind of unique, and I think it worked because the Service Club is a casual sort of club, and because of Yukinoshita's and Yuigahama's personalities.

"I think once they run, they won't come back," I said.

"I dunno…" As Yuigahama said that, she gave up on squeezing Yukinoshita and just started massaging her shoulders instead as a compromise. But Yukinoshita still seemed a little annoyed.

Let's not do that in front of guests, okay, guys?

To distract the judo club guys' attention, I said to Shiroyama, "So what? Do you think the guys who've left will come back?"

"…I doubt it." Shiroyama seemed to consider that possibility a moment, but then he shook his head slightly.

Yeah. I get the feeling that with sports clubs, once you quit, you're unlikely to come back. The reasoning there is different from that of a more casual club like ours. These athletic-type clubs operate based on a unique set of values—like their hierarchical structure, and group cohesion. That's their virtue but also their vice.

The word *bonds* can also mean *shackles*.

That very friendship is why you'll view them in an especially critical way once they're gone. If someone leaves and comes back, you might feel like they're traitors. And if the reason they left was because of harsh training from a former student, they probably wouldn't return to the club so long as that issue went unresolved.

"…Whatever the case, we have to actually see the situation, or we can't say anything," said Yukinoshita.

"Yeah. And some people can handle more than others. For now, let's just see you guys train," I agreed. There was the possibility that maybe this graduate's rigorous training was not actually a big deal, and the ones who had quit were hopeless wimps. Some of the guys had put up with it and stayed on, after all.

The first of the remnants still toughing it out, Shiroyama, nodded. "Roger. He won't be coming today, so how about tomorrow?"

I had no plans on either day, so I left the decision to Yukinoshita. I looked over at the girls to ask what we'd do, and Yuigahama must have had no objections, as she looked at Yukinoshita, too.

Yukinoshita replied, "Yes, I don't mind."

"Then see you guys tomorrow," Yuigahama said next, and she raised her hand.

"Thank you." Pota-yama bowed politely, and with the other two potatoes following, they left the clubroom.

I watched the three go, then looked out the window.

The summer had just begun, and the sun remained high even in the evening. The blazing sun made me think the judo dojo had to be pretty hot.

It was the day after Shiroyama and the judo club guys had visited the Service Club.

The three of us decided to take a peek at the judo club practice.

The dojo was on the first floor of the gymnasium building. It had windows at floor level, maybe for airflow, so we could circle around from outside to sneak a peek.

The term *high school sports clubs* calls to mind a lively image. The scattering sweat. The shrill cries. And the tears of emotion. The sort of coming-of-age graffiti you imagine scrawled on the walls of their youth.

But the reality was different.

The sweat was wrung from them, the shrieks sounded rather dark, and the tears were just tears. The few judo club members there were working so hard, you'd think they were ready to vomit blood.

They don't look like they're having fun at all...

The biggest cause of this seemed to be that former student. He was this one particularly stern guy in a judo uniform, and his stature clearly differentiated him from the other club members. He stood boldly at the head of the room, watching the club members practice.

But all they were practicing was running.

Shiroyama, the two guys from the day before, and a few others were running endless loops around the dojo. *Is running something you have to do for judo?* I didn't know much about it, but it seemed to me that running in this sweltering hot dojo in the middle of what I'd call a heat wave was rough treatment.

Mr. Graduate glanced at the clock and slowly stood. "That's enough. Those of you who were too slow, keep running for the seconds you went over. The rest of you, we're starting sparring." And then without any time for a break, they began training.

"Whoa, he's tough on them...," Yuigahama peeked in from behind to say.

"Yes, it does look severe. I have to wonder about it from a health and safety perspective...," Yukinoshita added, stuck close behind Yuigahama.

Though I did have some doubts, like Yukinoshita had mentioned, so far it looked surprisingly legitimate. No way I wanted to do it, though. All you had to say was *strict sports club*, and I was out.

I guess it's a little different from what I assumed, I thought as I watched for a little while longer, but then once they started attack practice, the mood clearly changed.

"You suck! Go run laps until you die!" he yelled at them, his tone violent. "You won't learn anything if you can't even pull off one attack! This is how my seniors taught me. You have to learn it with your body, or you won't get it!"

He continued to beat them down with his moves.

"You'll never make it out there if you start whining over this! High school clubs are easy. The world out there is far harsher than this!"

His lectures went on and on.

Me, Yukinoshita, and Yuigahama all fell silent.

Frankly speaking, this felt like a different dimension to me. I'm sure there are probably clubs out there that are stricter, harsher, and more unfair than this judo club. But the oddest thing of all was that the club submitted to their senior without a single complaint.

I didn't enjoy watching either party here.

I take it for granted that any person, any living creature, would avoid things they don't like, and if they don't, I question it. This was why I couldn't blame the people who'd left this situation. Blaming the people who left was the problem here, I'd say.

With this, my plan to call back the original club members evaporated.

"I've seen enough," I said, moving away from the window and checking with the other two. They both nodded, and we turned around and started heading for the clubroom.

At the end, I turned back just one more time.

I could only barely see Shiroyama through the window, practicing in silence. I forced myself to turn away, then started following the others back to the clubroom.

Anyway, we knew what was going on with the judo club. Now I just had to think up a way to deal with it.

X   X   X

Once we were back in the clubroom, I finally relaxed. After being outside, getting back into the cool made me acknowledge how comfortable this place was.

This must be how an office worker feels after coming back from running outside errands during summertime: like his workplace is heaven. Once he reaches that point, he's been broken in as a corporate slave. *Quick, get me an interview with an employment medical advisor.*

While drinking the ice-cold MAX Coffee I'd bought on the way back to the clubroom, I started by trying to sort out our impressions of the judo club. "So what do you guys honestly think?"

"It's hard to say... I don't have a point of reference from watching any other judo clubs, but it didn't seem very healthy to me," Yukinoshita said carefully after some thought, choosing her words.

A study for comparison is indeed an important element, but I feel like the idea that something is okay just because other people are doing it is unsound. I figured I could assume her opinion included this.

Yuigahama's answer, on the other hand, was simplicity itself. "I really couldn't handle that..." Though her remark was brief, it contained a depth of meaning. Was she talking about competitions, or about the members, or about the graduate, or watching them practice? You couldn't say which it was in a single word, but most likely, her statement included all those in general.

"What about you, Hikki?" Yuigahama asked.

My answer was a simple one. "I don't like it."

I've never had much of anything to do with athletics. You know, since it requires teamwork and stuff. So that means my knowledge of sports isn't deep, and my understanding is shallow. So I can't really have an opinion about it, but the one thing I can say is, the way the Soubu High School judo club operates does not align with my values.

"How rare for us to share the same perspective." As Yukinoshita said, all three of us had negative impressions. So much the better for moving things along.

"His request was to help them recruit more members, but…" Yuigahama reconfirmed this point. That was all Shiroyama had come to speak with us about, and we had accepted no other task. In other words, this was our greatest priority.

"Well then, I guess we have to canvass for some members," I said.

"I suppose we'll have to fix their image first," said Yukinoshita.

We had to communicate that the sport of judo itself, and not just Soubu High School's judo club, was a good and beneficial thing, or it would be difficult to gather new members now. So it was reasonable to treat the improvement of their image as a vital part of the plan.

As we were all setting our minds to this matter, Yuigahama suddenly clapped her hands. "Oh, what if we advertise that, like, judo will get you girls?"

Lame…

Yuigahama's eyes were kind of sparkling as she said that, but what a cheap idea…

"Would you believe that?" I argued her down on the spot.

"…Forget I said that." Immediately, Yuigahama withdrew her opinion, and she dejectedly slumped into her chair again.

Whenever you're starting something, immediately someone will bring up *It'll get you girls!* as a reason to do it. But consider this rationally. Playing some sport or joining a band will not get you girls.

The kind of guys who get girls don't need to do anything special to succeed. In fact, they don't have to do anything at all. Unpopular guys will have realized that fact, so that lure will have no effect.

As I was considering other types of hooks, Yukinoshita breathed out a little sigh. "Hmm, what about saying it will help you diet?"

"Those guys are the aggressively athletic type. For them, eating is a part of practice…," I argued. For high-impact sports, your body is your tool of the trade. That's why they eat lots to build strong muscles and meet calorie requirements. I hear in the sports world, being able to eat a lot is also a talent.

Yuigahama made a face, too. "And it'd make them all muscly…" Judging from her reaction, promising them bigger muscles wouldn't be a good idea, either… In fact, if you were looking to hook guys who want to get ripped, wouldn't it be best to offer all-you-can-drink protein shakes or something?

We couldn't quite come up with any ideas that struck us as *it*. As the three of us folded our arms and groaned, all we got was the passage of time.

Right about when the long hand of the clock had moved about ninety degrees, Yukinoshita unfolded her arms and stretched a little, like a cat that had gotten sick of napping. That seemed to get her thoughts on a new track. "So what we must do is not merely improve their image but fundamentally transform it," she concluded.

Now that she'd said that, it was reason enough to give up. That was a hopeless task, too. I'm sure VIPs in the judo world have thought long and hard about this, so there was no way we could come up with anything in such a short time. And even if we did think up something innovative, with no support behind it, it was unlikely we had enough power to get it to sink in.

"You can't undo people's stereotypes so easily," I said.

"Hmm…then for now, I guess we just try recruiting people the hard way?" Yuigahama moaned.

Well, that would be the straightforward solution. But just because it was the straightforward choice didn't mean it was the right one.

"Just trying to get people to join isn't gonna make them come. If that would work, then new members would be flooding in already." I think quite a few guys out there are interested in judo, but to actually do it, they'd have to have a reason or some external pressure that pushed them into it, or they'd be unlikely to take that step. "Plus, joining partway through the year is a lot to ask."

"…Maybe you're right." That seemed to convince Yuigahama, as she answered with a little nod.

Everything is like that.

Take part-time jobs, for instance. When everyone else already knows one another, it's just scary. They say those parties are for the newbies on the job, but they'll actually just have fun without you. What's with that? Is this some kind of roundabout way of saying, like, *There's no seat for your ass anyway!?* That's why I tactfully quit right away, you know!

It's scary to join in partway, and not just for social reasons. There's other stuff, too. "There's also, like… With sports, it's always clear who's better than who, so that'll give a lot of guys second thoughts," I said.

Yukinoshita folded her arms again and *hmm*'d. "So what you're saying is, we must emphasize that they can get better right away."

"More like that they can avoid embarrassing themselves by joining now."

"Oh, maybe you're right," said Yuigahama. "When everyone else is amazing, you can't help but feel depressed about it…"

Thank you for the agreement. Yuigahama has the tendency to pay too much attention to how others react, so maybe that's why she picked up on that psychological principle so easily. Very helpful.

By contrast, Yukinoshita seemed blown away by this, as if this was the first she'd ever learned of such a fact. "I see. As expected of Hikigaya, who falls behind no one when it comes to falling behind. What keen insight."

"Hey? Watch how you say that? I actually excel more than you think?" I excel so hard that I figured things out at that job pretty fast. So fast, in fact, that they talked smack about me behind my back. *He's not even cute, huh?*

But there would be no use in pointing that out as Yukinoshita began to get to the point. "So then we must suggest to the student body that the judo club is generally incompetent and not a big deal, while also coming up with a visible way to canvass for new members in the middle of the year."

She's right, but what a horrible way to say it…

She'd made clear the tasks we had to accomplish, but we were still far from a solution. Our narrower focus had resulted in more boxes to check off before our mission was complete. It wasn't gonna be easy to fulfill all of those. Would it be best to solve each of them as different issues?

Whatever the case, I figured the question was how we would promote judo. But I felt like *incompetent* and *worth joining* were mutually exclusive.

As I was considering all these things, Yuigahama suddenly raised her hand. "Oh! Oh, oh, oh!"

"...Yes, Yuigahama?" Yukinoshita must have been annoyed by the repeated exclamations, as she pointed at the other girl with some exasperation.

For some reason, Yuigahama stood up and broke into a big smile. "What about an event? There are a lot of *inkare*-style casual clubs out there that do events to get people interested." Yuigahama was babbling away, apparently tremendously excited. I could understand her fine, except for one unfamiliar word.

It seemed Yukinoshita had the same problem. "*In...kare*? ... Curry?" She tilted her head inquisitively.

I was curious about that word, too. "Like, is it short for 'Indian curry'?" It would be a great name for a curry restaurant. *CoCoICHI, Inkare, Karekichi. Oh hey, this* inkare *thing sounds like a topic a certain curry-loving voice actor would enjoy.*

Yuigahama shook her head hard at our reactions. "No! It's short for...in...inter? Collegiate! I think," she mused, her confidence waning.

Yukinoshita understood what she meant. "Intercollegiate—meaning, between universities? I believe the term refers to exchange at the university level, though..."

As expected of Yukipedia. She had the proper word registered in there. And *intercollegiate* was shortened as *inkare*.

After hearing Yukinoshita's explanation, Yuigahama moved on, talking animatedly. "Yeah, yeah! Sometimes casual clubs from a bunch of different universities will get together to do a thing. Since it's hard for them to get enough people if it's only from that one school, they do all kinds of events. I hear they often invite high schoolers, too."

Yuigahama sounded so casual about what was a rather frightening topic of discussion... *What? University students always do stuff like that? That's more than just devotion to having a good time. If they're even getting high school kids to come, then ew no what the hell yikes. This intercollegiate stuff sounds like a real den of Chads and Stacys (in my totally biased opinion). Does Yuigahama go to these, too?*

It must have come out on my face how totally put off I was. I might have even said *ew* out loud. Yuigahama noticed and flushed bright red, then panicked and got defensive. "I—I haven't gone myself! I just heard from a girl from another school!"

I couldn't just take her at her word, though, so I shot her a doubting look. Yuigahama quietly averted her eyes before adding in a mosquito-pitch murmur, "And, like, it's too scary to go to something like that..."

Well, I think you don't have to go, really. Hearing about it will stir unnecessary anxieties in certain people.

Now that I'd gotten my hate for these intercollegiate clubs out of my system, my mood brightened a bit. Actually, if that really worked to get people together, it could be a useful reference. "What kind of events do they do?" I asked.

Thinking back and *hmm*ing as she recalled, Yuigahama answered, "If it's a tennis club, for example, they'll have, like, a casual tennis tournament open to people who aren't experienced with tennis, or a bowling tournament, or a barbecue."

"Bowling...huh? What kind of club did you say?"

"Uh, tennis. Like I said."

Why would a tennis club have to go bowling...? Do you have to practice the wrist snap or something in order to do the perfect swing or something?

Intercollegiate clubs are scary after all.

Yuigahama ignored my shuddering and continued her explanation. "So we could do a judo tournament or something for fun, and then we'd have people from the judo club participate, like, casually."

I see. Fun.

If you say you're doing judo for fun, that'll pique the interest of some of the guys and get them to come. And if the judo club guys could take it easy on them and try to show them a good time, they could avoid giving the impression that the new guys suck in comparison.

That might actually be a great idea.

As I was starting to come around to the idea, Yukinoshita was nodding along as she mulled it over. But then her head stopped moving.

"But will the school give permission...?" She had no objection to the idea itself; her concern was about execution.

But that was probably nothing to worry about. "I think it'll be okay. This school is pretty lax when it comes to club activities." There's the Service Club, and even weird, nonsensical clubs like the UG Club.

Plus, some proper clubs are allowed to hold various functions, too. The tea ceremony club often has tea parties, and they invite non-members to their mini-events and stuff.

Yukinoshita seemed to understand what I was getting at, but her stern expression remained in place. "It seems we can manage soliciting people...but if they come with the goal of having fun, won't they end up quitting in the end?"

"...Probably," I answered frankly.

Yuigahama looked exasperated. *"'Probably'...?"*

But of course I was going to be frank, because I'd already anticipated that response. If even the members who'd enrolled at the start of the school year wanted to quit, then the new members were even more likely to quit. So we had to do something to prevent that.

"That's why you also have to change the environment." I didn't have to say what that referred to for Yukinoshita to figure it out.

"You mean to take that graduate out of the picture."

Correct. I answered with a nod.

This cycle would continue so long as we did not remove the cause. And what's more, the club's bad reputation would spread, making it so no one would even touch the judo club anymore.

The answer was clear, but something about this was bothering Yuigahama. She was holding her head with a complicated expression. "But I don't think the judo club guys would help us do that. Mainly the captain..."

"Indeed," said Yukinoshita. "It seems they admire him."

"That's less admiration and more blind worship, isn't it?" I said. *And I doubt Shiroyama feels that sort of blind worship only toward that one guy. I think that's the way he sees social hierarchy and group cohesion in general. He takes the unfairness as a given.*

History class has taught me plenty about just how difficult it is to make someone abandon their faith. That was why I figured we couldn't look to Shiroyama to cooperate with us. He hadn't even suggested getting rid of that graduate as an option.

"A way to eliminate him without the help of the judo club...," I muttered, and Yukinoshita slowly closed her eyes.

Yuigahama, on the other hand, was leaning back on her chair, making it creak as she rocked it back and forth and stared up at the ceiling.

Then as her head dropped back down, she stuck up a finger and opened her mouth. "We could tell some other teachers or the school board!"

"The school wouldn't want us exposing issues, either," I said. Our school does have a fairly prestigious reputation. If we had trouble with the coaching of a club here, it would be a big deal. If we tattled, there would be a superficial inquiry, they would insist there was no problem, they would announce as much, and then it'd be shelved forever.

It seemed Yukinoshita wasn't into that plan, either; her face showed her reluctance. "Yes. Most likely all they would do is give the club advisor a verbal warning."

"Worst case, the whole judo club would get blamed and shut down," I agreed.

There was also the possibility that the school wouldn't even see it as a problem in the first place. If what was going on was judged to be within the realm of regular instruction, then complaining would have the opposite effect and make everything worse.

Since this was a martial arts club, a little bit of danger was a given. Moreover, it was totally possible that he was keeping safety in mind with this coaching and that us amateurs would be evaluating it slightly differently from the experts.

It would be best not to make that dangerous bet.

"Then all we can do is make that guy leave of his own free will," I said. Leaving any uncertain elements out of the calculation, that was the best plan.

That was it, but both Yuigahama and Yukinoshita looked doubtful.

"But he wouldn't listen to what outsiders say, right?" Yuigahama gave a somewhat confused smile.

Yukinoshita's smile was more exasperated. "We'd have to bring in someone with even more status than the club advisor or that graduate—if that's even possible."

I was sure Yukinoshita was being somewhat ironic, but that was, in fact, our only option. "So then let's bring 'em in."

"Huh?" Yuigahama's eyes widened.

Yukinoshita started a little, giving me a look of doubt. "You don't even have any acquaintances, never mind friends. Do you have any prospects?"

The second sentence would have been enough. Why'd you have to go to the trouble of adding that? Well, it is true, though.

Gathering my thoughts bit by bit, I put together the words. "I do have prospects. Or I'm gonna make some now. In fact, we should hold an event to make it happen."

"Are you gonna invite someone to the event? But who?" Yuigahama asked, leaning forward with deep interest.

I gave a nasty smirk and told them the answer I'd come to. "The greatest outsider in the world—society."

Following my statement, Yuigahama made this *huuuuh* sound that didn't tell me if she really understood or not. *Was that a little too complicated...?*

But Yukinoshita cracked a smile. She got it. "It's ultimately not any acquaintance of yours, is it?"

...I guess you're right. It's like I just know them, and they don't know me.

X X X

The next day, we began efforts to actualize this event.

First, we explained the plan to Shiroyama and all the others of the judo club. This part wasn't that hard. We just said it would be a big event to generate some buzz and draw in members, which was easy enough to understand.

But we did not at all touch on our ulterior plan. We didn't want to deal with resistance from them, and no matter what our intentions were, ultimately, I would have that graduate leave of his own free will. There was no need to bother telling them.

After we'd explained things to the judo club, we negotiated with the school. We'd be inviting all the students to participate in the judo tournament, so of course the teachers would ask us a few questions about our plans. It would be a pain to have the school getting in the way further down the line, so discussing plans beforehand would make our future operation smoother.

To negotiate, first, we went to the judo club advisor—though *we* didn't really include me. Shiroyama was the one to explain the whole thing about doing a demonstration to gather members. As expected, even though the guy was just a decorative advisor, he'd been concerned about the recent loss of members, too, so we were able to get permission with no issue. He gave us some basic instructions on safety considerations, but having the judo club members on hand to oversee everything cleared that hurdle. The venue would be the martial arts dojo, too, so there was nothing to worry about on that front.

So far, it was all going well.

Now for the participants.

I had to enter myself, so I'd have to get some team members as well. More importantly, however, I had to secure the minimum number of participants necessary in order to hold the event at all.

Right away, Yukinoshita put together some tournament outlines. She printed stacks of them and stuck them up all over, then got the judo club guys help us out to distribute them everywhere.

But we couldn't expect much out of this approach to advertisement. The orchestra club and tea ceremony club often used notice boards and flyers to promote their events, but the participation rate for those wasn't that high. Generally, for these events, you get people to come by using your personal connections.

And if we're talking about connections, then me and Yukinoshita couldn't help there. Plus, the judo club network was weakened, so we couldn't expect much from them, either. Our remaining option,

Yuigahama, wouldn't have enough personal connections on her own to put a tournament together.

So then we had to explore a more effective, more efficient avenue.

What's the greatest audience draw for events?

Casting.

Of course, content is often relevant, but since this was a judo tournament, and novelty wasn't a major element here, we'd have to have something else to win people over. And fortunately, I had in mind someone in the school with a great ability to draw people in.

Yuigahama and I—mostly Yuigahama, really—went to negotiate.

During lunch hour, classroom 2-F was always abuzz with chatter. With summer vacation so close, the energy during lunch hour was especially high. On that day, I decided not to go outside, either, and remained inside the classroom.

This was to book the shocking participation of Hayato Hayama in the Soubu High School judo tournament: the S1 Grand Prix. I made up that name just now, if you were wondering.

Hayama had been able to gather a fair-sized audience even for that impromptu grass tennis match a while back. For an event like this one, with prior notice, we could expect an even greater turnout than last time. He was a must-have.

But even saying that, the main negotiator here would be not me but Yuigahama.

"'Kay, I'm gonna try talking to him." After going to buy a bun for lunch, we had a little meeting before Yuigahama cheerfully returned to her clique. Watching her go, I sat down in my own seat.

Now then, I would observe with the utmost attention, ears alert as I ate. If Yuigahama was having trouble, then I'd make sure to back her up indirectly. Easier said than done.

As I listened, Yuigahama immediately brought up the topic with Hayama and the gang. "Oh, so I heard the judo club is gonna be holding this judo tournament."

"Hmm." Miura munched on a bun as she showed absolutely no interest. At least she was making listening noises despite her lack of interest; maybe she kinda was a good person.

Still, seeing her with a bun in one hand and cell phone in the other, I was on the edge of my seat waiting for her to chomp into her cell phone by mistake. *Don't be on your phone while you're eating, okay? And with other people, too. Only us loners are allowed to be on our phones while eating, you know?*

Not discouraged by Miura's attitude, Yuigahama continued. "It's like, um, *Let's see who's the strongest in the school!* That kinda thing?"

"Oh, now that you mention it, I did see that flyer." Hayama joined in the conversation without missing a beat. As expected of the guy who will actually listen to people and go along with the conversation, thereby maintaining social harmony.

Yuigahama had probably also been banking on this. She instantly turned the conversation toward Hayama. "You look like you'd enjoy that, Hayato! Why don't you join?"

It's like she's not even trying, with that invitation... Nothing about him suggests he would be good at this...

"Huh? D-do I?"

See? Thought so. He's a little confused, isn't he? Hayama has a reputation for being the pure and charming type, which is the polar opposite of judo.

Of course, I wasn't the only one with that opinion. "No way. Hayato doesn't come off like a judo guy at all." Tobe cackled wildly, and Yamato and Ooka laughed along with him.

Yuigahama moved in. "Oh, and you could do it, too, Tobecchi? You're kinda strong, aren't you? Not like I'd know. Why don't you and Hayato do it together? It's team matches, in groups of three."

"Huh? Judo might be kinda..."

Hmm. So her strategy was to start by filling in Hayama's moats, huh? Yuigahama had not broached this subject without a plan but rather had deliberately begun with an absurd proposition so as to make it easier to broach the subject with Tobe...probably. Maybe not. I also feel like she might just say things like that.

I didn't know how much of this was calculated. Then someone even more incalculable to me reacted with a twitch. "...Do it, together? J-judo? ...I like that!" As if she'd been ruminating over the choice of words, Ebina reacted slowly.

"Ebina. Here, a tissue." Miura tossed a tissue over to Ebina, who looked ready to spew blood from her nose at any moment.

Ebina thanked her and pressed the tissue to her nose but still continued passionately. "I like it! Judo's good!" Ebina gave a thumbs-up.

For some reason, Tobe suddenly began to approve, too. "Uhhh... judo might be kinda...kinda something I could do, huh?"

The nuance there is subtly different from before... Oh, Japanese. Such a difficult language...

"B-boys locked in a grapple and falling for each other? Who?! Which one is doing the falling, Hikitani?!"

Don't point me out specifically... I felt sharp eyes on me, so I jerked my gaze away. As I was looking the other way, negotiations steadily continued.

When I timidly turned around, Tobe was whacking Hayama on the back with newfound enthusiasm. "You come, too, Hayato!"

"Hmm, well, it's not something you often have the opportunity to try." Unsurprisingly, when he had Yuigahama and Tobe pushing him one after another, Hayama was unable to refuse. He was leaning more and more toward joining the tournament.

Was this the fate of the one who possessed *the Zone*? Once you've created an atmosphere, you are compelled to act in order to avoid destroying it.

And then the final nail was driven in.

"If you join, Hayato, I'll go watch." Now that Miura was finally making some show of interest, Hayama seemed to make up his mind.

"Then I guess I will," he answered with a charming smile.

Mission complete. Now we just had to spread the news that Hayama would be in the tournament, and that would grow the audience. And once the scale had grown, that should cause even more people to want to participate.

"Then maybe we'll join, too..."

"Yeah." There was an immediate ripple effect, as Yamato and Ooka both declared their participation.

At their core, boys like martial arts.

No, it's less that they like it and more that they have an interest. At some point in time, they would have wanted to hold the title of "the strongest." If you just have the right trigger, I don't think it's that hard to get them to remember that feeling.

Now it was settled. All four guys of Hayama's clique—Hayama, Tobe, Ooka, and Yamato—would be participating. What's more, Miura would be in the audience, too, so for Soubu High School, this was an all-star lineup.

Hayama suddenly realized something. "But it's in groups of three, huh…?" he muttered quietly, standing up. Then he strode away. I vaguely followed him with my eyes, and mysteriously, my eyes never moved.

Huh, he's coming toward me…

During the scant few seconds I was wondering if there was someone nearby Hayama would have wanted to talk to, he came toward me. And then he stopped right there and grinned, showing his white teeth. "Hikitani, will you join the judo tournament with me?"

What's he talking about, all of a sudden…?

Though my head understood his words, my heart couldn't. But he'd given me an invitation, so I had to give him a response of some sort. "Huh? Uh, you know, I'm like. Can't. 'Cause of reasons." If I'm invited to something, I immediately refuse. This is the correct response when someone acts out of politeness.

But Hayama did not back down. Without breaking his smile, he continued. "I see. Well, Tobe and the guys will be a group of three, so I'm gonna be left out."

"O-oh. Well, yeah…" I waffled as he looked weirdly straight at me.

Hayama shrugged his shoulders. "So how about it? …You're the one who recommended doing it this way, aren't you?"

Agh. I get it. He was talking about how we formed groups for the workplace tour a while back.

Back then, I had indeed suggested an arrangement that would separate Hayama from Tobe and their other friends. If they would be taking that suggestion this time, too, then Hayama wouldn't be in a group with them. Of course, just like last time, the baton would be passed to me.

So I was forced to accept his proposal. Most of all, it would be bad for us if my refusal were to cause Hayama to not participate. "...But we're still short one," I said by way of agreement.

Hayama smiled boldly. "Could you invite one more for me, then?"

"Uh, I don't have any friends I could invite." Obviously, it'd be faster for Hayama to invite someone. I implicitly shoved the task off on him, but he smoothly avoided that, too.

"What about that one guy?"

That one guy... Wait, was there someone? I thought, and then I hit on the answer. *O-oh. Totsuka!*

Now that we were on the same page, I said, "Oh...him, huh?"

"Yeah, yeah, Zaimokuza. He seems strong. I think he might be perfect."

Oh, him...

If that was Hayama's choice, then I couldn't not invite Zaimokuza. Hayama was a major element of this event. I had to meet his demands as best I could and make sure he enjoyed participating. *Guess I have no choice...*

My shoulders slumping in despair must have looked like a nod or something, as Hayama replied with a nod of his own. "Then thanks." With that, he returned to his seat.

Being on a team with Zaimokuza would be a disappointment, but this turn of events was in fact convenient for the Service Club. I'd only anticipated using Hayama as a mascot for drawing in the crowds, but if I could use him as a weapon, too, that would help me out.

Now my plans were set, to a degree.

All that was left was to determine how much of the details could be worked out beforehand, and whom the odds would favor in our big gamble on the day of the event.

X　X　X

The judo tournament was just for fun, just a bit of goofing around.

Or so we claimed, but the event had pulled in more participants and a greater audience than we expected.

Right before summer vacation might have been the perfect time for this. Soon, we would be away from school for a little over a month, so maybe this little diversion was a good last event to get excited about before the break.

The dojo wasn't all that big, so the presence of a standing audience told us the event was a success.

Shiroyama, on standby near the head of the dojo, scanned the whole scene. He didn't seem like the expressive type, but this time, apparently, he found this something to be impressed over. "I didn't think we'd get this many people. Thanks. You've been a big help."

He thanked us, but none of this would help anyone.

Our job was starting now—and I doubted he'd thank us after it was done.

So I didn't touch on that and instead brought up something else. "Anyway, that graduate is going to be coming today, right?"

"Yeah. I made sure to invite him, just like you said. I think he'll be here soon."

As long as he was coming, that was good. That was the one thing out of my power, so I'd had to rely on Shiroyama for that. His attendance was uncertain and, in fact, my biggest concern.

Thanks to Shiroyama, the graduate should be watching the tournament right from the start. How might he react? I didn't know what his views would be on doing judo for fun. "Did he say anything about this?"

"…No. But he didn't seem particularly angry." Shiroyama appeared to be recalling his exchange with the graduate, making sure he was speaking accurately. For now, the graduate wasn't opposed to this. The guy was taking the trouble to come back to a club he'd retired from. I'd been worried he might prefer they remain exclusive, but it seemed that wasn't the case, at least.

Well, this event was basically being held under the pretext of attracting new members. Maybe that was why he would let it go.

"I see, then that's good," I said. "We have to show him you're all really trying hard to breathe some life back into the club."

"…Yeah." Shiroyama suddenly seemed shy. His face was potato-like to begin with, so it was real hard to tell, though.

"Well, I hope it goes well for you. Later, then," I said to Shiroyama, walking up from the back of the dojo to the entrance.

A long table had been set up there as reception for the entering teams. Currently, Yuigahama was sitting there, zoning out. Behind her, drawing up a tournament chart on some poster board was Yukinoshita.

In all, there would be eight teams in the tournament. Aside from the team of me, Hayama, and Zaimokuza, and the team the judo club was having compete, everyone else was on a first-come, first-serve basis until we were full. If we allowed too many people, we wouldn't be able to handle them all. More importantly, it would slow things down.

The more fun you're having, the shorter the time feels, so maybe keeping the tournament short and dense would make it more fun. It was a paradoxical way to stage the show.

Also, if it ended up being, y'know, super-boring, ending it quickly would provide its own sort of joy...

"Just about time to start, huh?" I said to Yuigahama, who was on her phone like she had nothing to do.

Without raising her head, she answered, "Yeah. I think everyone'll probably come once Hayato's here?"

I recalled that Hayama had said he was slipping out of his soccer club practice to do this. It wasn't a problem, since I was on his team and I was here, and I'd registered Tobe's team, too. Now we just had to await their arrival.

I glanced over at the tournament chart.

Yukinoshita was filling out the names of the teams that had entered. The judo club team was positioned right opposite ours.

So we wouldn't compete until the finals.

"Hikigaya." Yukinoshita seemed to notice me behind her and spoke to me without turning around.

"Hmm?"

"I did place you at either end like you said, but you still have to win your way up, or things won't go according to plan, right?"

"...Yeah, that's right."

"...Yet another shaky plan..." Yukinoshita breathed an exasperated sigh.

But it wasn't like I had no plan at all here. "If we lose, we'll run an exhibition match or something. We can still make it work. It'd just change how we do it, not what we'd be doing."

"All right… It just leaves a bad taste in my mouth." Yukinoshita drew the last line with a squeak of her marker and finally turned around. Then she grinned wide. "But even if it's not me personally, I wouldn't like my club having a blot on its record. So if you're going to lose, I'd at least like for you to do it well."

"Don't assume I'm gonna lose…" She was wearing down my motivation before the match had even started. *Why does she smile when she says stuff like this?*

Well, it was true it didn't matter if we lost.

We were holding this event, and the graduate was coming, so the plan had an 80 percent chance of coming together, regardless.

It wasn't a lie that this was a PR event for recruiting new club members, but that was just one side.

The other purpose was to get rid of that graduate.

And to that end, he needed to lose his authority. I had to hurt him badly enough he would struggle to show his face here at school again. I'd come up with a number of methods for accomplishing that, but since I couldn't say they would have no effect on the judo club down the road, I had to take that into consideration, too.

The smartest thing to do would be to have the graduate join in this tournament and then lose the match. But that really seemed unrealistic. This guy had gotten into university on a judo sports recommendation, so it'd be safe to assume that an amateur couldn't beat him. Which led us to plan B.

"It's just about time…," Yukinoshita said as she checked the clock. Following her eyes, I looked over to see it was indeed about time to start.

With perfect timing, the entrance area burst into loud chattering. It seemed Hayama and his friends had arrived.

"I'm getting so pumped!" I could hear Tobe's voice above the rest. I looked toward the sound to see Miura and Ebina among the others with him.

Hayama, at the center of their group, noticed me and quickly rushed over. "Sorry we're late."

"No, you're right on time." I pointed at the clock, and Hayama breathed a sigh of relief.

"I see; that's good. Also, he's here, too." Hayama turned around, and there was a guy glancing around suspiciously, looking like a bear wandered down into the city.

"Nghnn... What is all this commotion?" He put his hand to his mouth, occasionally making suspicious *herp derp* noises.

"You're late," I addressed Zaimokuza when he showed no indication of coming in.

Zaimokuza twitched, tense as a mouse about to bolt for the wall. But then when he realized I was the one addressing him, he gradually relaxed. "Ngh, 'tis Hachiman! Upon your summons, I leaped forth to appear and see, but what is this?"

"Oh, it's a tournament. You're competing. On my team."

"Uh? Hey?! Mr. Hachiman?!" He wailed his incomprehension.

But wait, he never got an explanation? Oh well. "Anyway, the competition is starting, so hurry up and let's go."

"Herk! A competition?!" Zaimokuza groaned, looking right and left, then at the tournament sheet right in front of him. "Herm...at least tell me what sort of tournament this is... If 'twere a duel, I could manage somehow, but..."

"It's something like that. It's a Japanese-style duel."

"No, I know thou lieth..." I could see Zaimokuza was starting to gush sweat, but I prodded him in the back, conveying us into the dojo.

On the way, Hayama approached us, too, pushing Zaimokuza together with me. He's a good guy. Although I think a *really* good guy probably wouldn't have been pushing people at all. "Let's do this, Zaimokuza." Ever breezy, Hayama prodded Zaimokuza along as he greeted the other boy.

"Y-yeah..." Zaimokuza, on the other hand, was an eternally overheated human tropical rain forest. He didn't even give Hayama a decent answer. "Who? Whassisface Hayama...," he muttered.

Well, regardless, we had the whole team here.

I shifted my gaze over to the reception to see Yuigahama making a big O with her arms. Guess all the other teams were here, too. I looked over at the tournament bracket to see Yukinoshita nod, then point to her own watch. We were a little behind schedule, but it seemed everyone was ready to go.

At last, I glanced to Shiroyama, up at the back of the dojo.

He seemed not to notice my eyes. He was talking with the graduate, who'd just arrived. Instead, the first-year potato crew, Tsukui and Fujino, greeted me with little *heys*.

Now all the actors were in place.

Finally, the curtain was rising on the S1 Grand Prix, the tournament to decide the strongest in Soubu High School...

X X X

Shiroyama, the ceremonial organizer for the event, gave a brief opening speech. He spoke as simply as ever, but the audience was full of enthusiastic types who cheered wildly for him anyway.

Then, without much delay, the first match began. This one was between the judo club and some guys I didn't really know. The judo club had an easy victory in a lighthearted match, and that vibe was probably why the second and third also went by with a good energy. Tobe's team, which was in the second match, also safely moved their token to top four. Well, there were only eight teams, so we were all in the top eight to begin with.

We went through the scheduled matches one by one until we reached the fourth. This was our first sortie.

Now changed into a borrowed judo uniform, I headed out to the square battlefield at last.

On the way there—I found Zaimokuza moaning nonstop. "Hachiman...? Hey...what is this...?"

"Shut up, I told you—it's judo," I replied, and Zaimokuza turned a reproachful gaze on me.

"You told me 'twas a Japanese-style duel..."

"It's...you know. It's like, I figured it'd be good reference for your novel."

"Herm...I see." I'd just spouted out the first thing that came to mind, but that actually seemed to convince Zaimokuza, and he nodded with a *fngggh. Uhhh, that's not a normal sound of agreement, though.*

But it seemed I'd managed to flip Zaimokuza's M-2 attention-seeking switch. Or maybe he was just so nervous in front of such a crowd he'd lost his marbles. He'd switched gears into Master Swordsman General mode, so he wouldn't be bothered by how people saw him anymore. Another dark chapter in the life of Zaimokuza...

We lined up on the mats.

Working as judge was one of the judo club potatoes...Tsukui? Or was it Fujino? I think they had to be taking turns doing it. I'm not sure, but that was probably what was happening.

As instructed by the judge, both teams bowed to each other, then backed away, except for their first-round competitor. It seemed the other team had already decided their order.

"Who goes when?" I asked. Order was a part of strategy. This tournament wasn't a knockout competition but rather a round robin. The first team to two victories would win.

I'd been addressing Hayama, but for some reason, Zaimokuza answered. "Herm, I would be first. I shall not yield the honor of point warrior."

"I suppose that's fine." Being a mature guy, Hayama dealt with Zaimokuza's sudden fit in an extremely humane manner. "Then I'll go second. Hikitani, we'll be counting on you to be the boss."

"You okay with that?" *I'm not wearing a construction helmet or anything, though. Maybe I should get fatter and fuzzier.*

"I'm at my best in a position with less pressure. Zaimokuza, you can do it," Hayama said with a smile and a light pat on Zaimokuza's back.

"U-uh, okay." Just that casual interaction with Hayama had already gotten Zaimokuza worked up. He was starting to drip with sweat.

Just how nervous are you—or do you like Hayama?

"Sorry to ask this of you so suddenly. Thanks," I said to him.

"Oh, no need for such formality! You leave this to me!" For some reason, Zaimokuza answered me boldly. Feeling I could rely on him, I patted him lightly on the back like Hayama had. It was slimy-slick. *…Huh? What is this guy, an amphibian? Is this sweat?* I wondered if he'd slathered himself with Vaseline. *Wow, Hayama,* I thought. He hadn't even winced. He really was amazing.

Once we left the mats, the first match began immediately.

As we watched, Zaimokuza moved far more quickly than I'd anticipated. But his opponent could also move around decently, and he quickly grabbed Zaimokuza's sleeve.

But instantly, the opponent's face twisted in fear and loathing. Despite having managed to grab a sleeve, he jerked his hand away and looked down at it in horror.

He'd fallen into…the Zaimokuza Swamp…

Zaimokuza took full advantage of that opening. He firmly grabbed the collar of his opponent and forcefully yanked him around. With their difference in weight, he tossed the opponent easily.

"P-point?" For some reason, the judge said it like a question.

The stir that ran through the audience was rather restrained. The applause was sparse, too.

But even so, a victory is a victory.

Zaimokuza strolled coolly back toward us. "How was that, Hachiman?"

"Incredible." Incredible amounts of sweat… *In a fairer world, you'd be executed for the illicit manufacture of salt. See, that judo club guy wiping the mat right now looks like he's suffering. Now I feel bad for him…*

"Then next is my turn, huh?" Hayama said, striding gallantly to the center of the mats. Instantly, an intense applause swelled, and then there was the Hayama call.

HA-YA-TO (whoo)! HA-YA-TO (soiya)! Over and over.

They must have revised the chant at some point; they were even adding gestures. *Come on, is everyone practicing this?*

"Hayatooo!"

One voice stood out particularly among the high-pitched cheers: Miura. She was waving a fan and cheering him on. She's surprisingly fangirlish, huh? After she was completely uninterested in the other matches, fanning herself the whole time and moaning about how it was so, sooo hot… Also, not like it matters, but Tobe's gestures were obnoxious.

Hayama met these cheers with confidence, casually raising a hand in reply. He was so overflowing with composure that it was revolting. Meanwhile, his opponent had been completely engulfed by the atmosphere.

Basically, victory was decided before the match had even begun.

And the match was over startlingly quickly. As soon as it started, Hayama took the opponent's hand for a beautiful one-arm shoulder throw. With the splitting cheers behind him filling the dojo, Hayama walked back to us like it was nothing. "Now we've won."

"Y-yeah…"

Frankly, I felt a little awkward about being included in that *we* when I hadn't even done anything, but anyway, victory was good.

Man, Hayama's a seriously high-spec guy… And yet, I hear a certain someone once beat this gentleman in a tennis match, you know? Well, even though I won the match, I lost the war… Still, I hardly did anything in that match, did I? If I can nab a victory without doing anything at all, then I should really not get a job.

But even if my plan was to avoid getting a job in the future, right here and now, I had a job to do.

"We still have some time before our next set. Go kill time however you like," Hayama said to Zaimokuza, and I left the two of them.

My feet took me to the head of the dojo.

The other matches were still ongoing. They were now in the first match of the semifinals, and the judo club and Tobe's team would be on. Hayama and Miura and their friends would be watching them together, while Zaimokuza would have turned into a statue with no place to go.

And the one at the head of the dojo was watching the match, too—with total boredom.

It was that judo club graduate. I didn't know his name. I didn't really care. I had no direct connection to him and no reason to show him respect as a senior, but I went out of my way to address him politely.

"Excuse me." I went up to the head of the dojo and stood beside him to strike up a conversation.

He turned to me, looking annoyed. Perhaps because I was an unfamiliar face, he looked momentarily confused, but he quickly covered that up and gave me a casual reply. "Hey."

Once he had responded, I continued. "What do you think of this new judo club venture?"

"…Yeah. I guess it's not bad. Once you're out of high school, you can't really play around like this, after all," he said as he fanned himself restlessly, as if trying to take up more space. I listened, digesting every word he said.

I get it—so this is what he talks like; this is what he acts like. Once I had made sure that my evaluation of him from what I'd seen at practice was correct, I said, "Really? Shiroyama came to us for help, so we thought up lots of ideas. We figured something fun like this was important. That's why we got all these people."

The graduate gave me a hard look, then blinked wide two, three times. "…Oh, so you did all the work to set this up? But just playing around won't do them any good, so don't spoil Shiroyama, all right? The world out there is harsher than you think. You have to practice and study hard now, or you're not gonna cut it." He closed the fan with a snap, and I resisted the urge to burst out laughing.

Instead, I said, "Oh, I know. Why don't you join the competition, too?"

"…Huh? O-oh… I'll think about it."

"Come in at any time, if you feel like it," I said, then left him.

There must have been something about the way I'd approached him that irritated him, as I felt his suspicious gaze following me, but I shook it off and walked away.

It was about time for our match—though the other guys on my team would probably win, so it didn't matter if I wasn't there.

On my way back, I ran into Shiroyama, who had just finished judging the match.

"…What were you talking about with him?" So Shiroyama had

seen me. We'd been at the head of the room, after all, and Shiroyama must have had his attention on the graduate, too.

"Nothing, really. Just having a meeting to discuss staging."

"Staging?" Shiroyama tilted his rustic head like a potato rolling to the side.

"Oh yeah. I should mention this to you, too. Me and him are going to have a match for the last round of the finals, so you act as judge."

"That's fine, but…"

"I'm counting on you for staging the show."

"Hmm?" Shiroyama tilted his head, a questioning look on his face.

X   X   X

In the end, I didn't join the semifinals, either. All I did was hand over a mop to the judo club guy to deal with Zaimokuza's sweat.

Zaimokuza and Hayama both won their fights, taking us up to the finals. Zaimokuza's slimy defense and Hayama's one-arm shoulder throw yet again were the clinchers. I'd come all this way without lifting a finger.

The judo club beat Tobe's team to become our opponents for the finals. I hadn't even noticed those guys lose.

By the way, since Shiroyama was club captain, he was staying out of the tournament as a handicap. Competing were Tsukui, Fujino, and one guy I didn't know and thus dubbed Japanese Yam.

While watching two of the Brothers Tuber start warm-ups out of the corner of my eye, we started getting ready for the finals.

That was when Yuigahama and Yukinoshita, who had just been watching from a distance, approached me.

"Do you need something? Be considerate; don't talk to me before matches," I said.

Seemingly unbothered by the heated atmosphere of the dojo, Yukinoshita replied coolly, "Then you're in a competition all year round, hmm?"

"Basically, yeah. So what?" I casually deflected her sarcasm, and Yuigahama responded with a raised hand in greeting.

"I figured we'd cheer you on at the end, at least."

"Oh. Thanks. Only if I go on, though," I said, looking over at Hayama and Zaimokuza. Those two might actually just win this thing.

"You will. Nothing will be resolved if you don't," Yukinoshita pressed, as if she could see through me. I actually wasn't sure how much Yukinoshita had figured out, but she sounded strangely and disconcertingly convincing.

Indeed, this was not yet over. "...Yeah."

"Yeah, yeah! Give it your best shot, for the judo club!" Yuigahama threw up her arms in a happy-go-lucky manner.

But I just couldn't get in on her enthusiasm, not sincerely. "It's not just for them."

"Huh?" With just a blank, innocent look, Yuigahama asked, "Then who is it for?"

But before I could answer, it was time for the match to begin.

X   X   X

From the very first round, the finals were a madhouse.

Five seconds after both parties bowed at the start:

"Doof."

Along with the fierce *bam* of impact came a plainer sound, like when you hit the wall in Dragon Quest.

When I looked to see what had happened, I discovered something like a washed-up sea lion lying there. Zaimokuza had been thrown. He didn't even twitch.

"Point!" was proclaimed loudly.

"Zaimokuza...lost...?" *I can't believe it. Zaimokuza has thus far prided himself in his unequaled strength, and yet, he lost so easily...* So he was the Yamcha here, huh?

"The judo club boys must be used to his type," Yukinoshita explained, having appeared to kneel next to me.

"Ngh! So the slime has backfired on him!"

"Gross..." Yuigahama added insult to injury. She was sitting beside Yukinoshita on her rear with her knees in front of her.

It's not good to kick corpses.

A judo club guy rolled away the fallen and still Zaimokuza. He was moist like a wet sponge, and his wake was like a slug's slime trail as they tossed him out.

In the meanwhile, the dojo was abuzz. Zaimokuza's dramatic and abrupt defeat had come as a shock. But once they were ready for the next match, the welling cheers drowned out those murmurs.

The shock of the first match was overshadowed by the Hayama call.

This was the finals, and Hayama's was the fight we absolutely could not afford to lose. A lot of competitions you "definitely can't afford to lose" end in a loss or a scoreless draw, but this one we *really* couldn't afford to lose. If Hayama lost the second match, that would mean we were over.

The audience just got even more excited. Ebina was cheering loud the whole time with an enormous grin, while Miura might strip if Hayama won…or so the boys hoped, given how excited she was. Did I mention Tobe was obnoxious?

"Hikitani." Hayama stood. His voice was not lost among the cheers; I could hear him clearly.

"Hmm?"

"You should warm up." The moment it left his mouth, Hayama had already started walking out. This declaration of victory, so very mild-mannered and yet so very arrogant, was unbearably Hayama. It was rather irritating, but he was about to win now, embarrassingly enough.

And then, right when Hayama walked out into the ring, the Hayama cyclone peaked, whipping the audience into a chaotic whirlpool.

Suddenly, Ebina was quiet. Right as I noticed this, I saw her lying down on Miura's lap with a wet handkerchief over her head. *What? What did she see? What is she thinking…?*

Finally, Hayama and his opponent faced each other.

That was when the dojo door flew open.

"Ahhh~! I finally found you~! Hayamaaa! Please come to club~!"

That stupid-sounding voice clashed entirely with the sense of tension in the dojo. Looking over, I saw a girl with blond shoulder-length hair wearing a pink tracksuit. Completely ignoring the mood, she marched straight for Hayama.

She disregarded everyone's astonishment without a care.

When Hayama saw the girl, he was uncharacteristically rattled.

"I-Iroha…"

"Hayama, the first-years don't know what to do with you gone."

"O-oh. Um, right now I'm a little busy." Hayama attempted to put his foot down harder, but this Iroha girl or whoever didn't listen at all and grabbed the sleeve of Hayama's judo uniform.

Huh? Who is that girl…? I thought.

From the audience, Tobe stood up and called out, "Sorry, Irohasu. I'll go back with you, so let Hayato off the hook."

"Nah, you can stay, Tobe."

Smoothly rejected with a smile, all Tobe could do was say "O-okay…" and sit back down again.

"Is that someone Hayama and Tobe know?" I asked, looking between Yukinoshita and Yuigahama.

Yukinoshita shook her head to indicate she didn't have an answer, but Yuigahama did happen to know. "Ohhh, that's Isshiki-chan. She's the soccer club manager, a first-year girl."

Oh-ho, Iroha Isshiki. Chii is learning—that that *is a hazard.*

…That thing is dangerous. That girl is absolutely dangerous. My ghost is whispering to me that you have to be careful of pretty, sweet, and gentle girls like that.

This Isshiki girl—this cute soccer club manager with a treacherous air about her—secured Hayama, then attempted to continue on out. She was just like a willful princess, and no one could reproach her.

"Shouldn't someone stop her?" The only one among us who thought to do something was Yukinoshita, but she didn't know what and so turned to me.

"Uh, I think we can just leave 'em."

"Can we?" she said doubtfully.

You've just been sitting there. You're not trying to make a move at all, are you?

But the ice queen's inaction to correct the princess's misconduct was no problem, since the other queen took action instead.

"Hey, you." Like the waves of heat from the ground in the midsummer, Miura rose. "Hayato's busy right now." Her tone could burn the earlobes of those who heard it.

But it was ineffective on the princess of the breeze. "Huh~? But the club needs him...," Isshiki argued back casually.

Miura kicked up the temperature a notch. *"What?"*

"H-hey, guys." Unsurprisingly, Hayama realized the situation was deteriorating and cut in between them, attempting to calm Miura. Isshiki delicately plucked at the hem of Hayama's shirt, trembling behind him.

That mouse-like gesture just raised Miura's hackles even more. She looked down, then sucked a deep breath in and out like a bellows and said, "Hayato, you go on to your club. I have to have a little chat with this girl."

"Huh?" Hayama's voice cracked, and he froze, staring at Miura's raised face.

"Go work hard at your club~. ♪"

This was probably the first time I'd ever seen Miura's ultimate smile.

Then she dragged Isshiki away. "Hayamaaaa!" Isshiki nearly shrieked, but Miura totally ignored her cries as she escorted her out.

Of course, Hayama couldn't just watch this happen, and he followed after them. "Sorry, Hikitani! I'll be right back!" he said, putting his hands together in apology to me, then rushed off.

Uh, there's no way you're coming back, though... Everyone's gonna be more interested in that off-site brawl now...

The crowd murmured, wondering what was going on.

Useless in the moment of truth... But he'd brought us to the finals, so we'd call that good enough.

The problem now was getting through the second round of this match.

"Wh-what's gonna happen?" Still sitting with her knees up in front of her, Yuigahama scooched toward me.

"We lose by default? Or maybe we move along the roster and have me go..."

"But then you'll have to forfeit the last one, so what's the difference?" Yuigahama was right. What would happen now?

As we were puzzling over this, a cool voice came from beside me. "It won't end up as a default."

Oh, as expected of Yukipedia. She was knowledgeable on the rules of judo.

"All we have to do is have me compete," she said, getting to her feet.

Uh, that's ridiculously arbitrary... "Uh, I don't think you can do that."

"Yeah, you're a girl." Yuigahama and I both attempted to stop her.

But Yukinoshita wasn't listening. "I don't recall ever setting any such requirements for participation. And it's not an official tournament. You don't mind, do you?"

"I do mind! You can't! No way!" Despite Yukinoshita's logic, Yuigahama made her feelings so abundantly clear, even Yukinoshita winced a little.

Well, there was no need to force Yukinoshita to compete now.

Though the opponent was in judo club, it looked like he was in first year, like a Chinese yam or Japanese yam or something. I could probably manage him. Glancing over to check, I saw the potato in question huddled with the other two having a secret talk. Then he looked over at Yukinoshita and gave a little blush.

...Oh-ho. Setting your sights high, Potato.

"I'll go out first," I said. "Hayama might come back before then." It seemed unlikely, but that was a better plan. I started getting to my feet, but Yukinoshita yanked my sleeve, and my head whipped back. "Erfh, ow... What?" I coughed at the unexpected attack.

Yukinoshita stared at me even more directly than usual. "What point would there be in that?"

"Huh?" I wanted to ask what she meant. My sour look did the asking for me, and Yukinoshita answered dispassionately and calmly.

"This is *your* shoddy plan. Didn't you set this up so that you could draw the graduate out in the final round?"

"…"

She had a point. We'd spent all this time planning out this event for the sake of luring out that graduate to this stage. Considering the effort we'd expended to get here, it would be a foolish decision to drop it all now.

This plan would work most effectively precisely because the ultimate stage had been set. So the safest plan among our remaining options would be for Yukinoshita to go out now.

Yukinoshita's cold gaze had cooled my head, and what she said next was like another splash of cold water. "Besides, you don't have to concern yourself with me." With a determined smile, she fixed a glare at her future opponent. "Essentially, all I have to do is keep him from ever laying a finger on me."

"…Is that the question here?! …At least… At least get changed?" Yuigahama protested tearfully, having abandoned trying to talk Yukinoshita out of this.

Yukinoshita nodded with a *hmm* of apparent agreement. "Fair enough."

"Okay, let's go!" Once that was decided, Yuigahama acted fast. She grabbed Yukinoshita's hand and immediately rushed off, only to return in fewer than ten minutes.

Yuigahama flopped down, exhausted, and for some reason, she looked like a mess. Yukinoshita, on the other hand, was crisp and dashing. She wore a white martial arts top tucked into red *hakama* pants. Her hair was tied up—in a bun, in fact, just like it had been the day before.

"Why's she dressed like that…?" I asked.

"We borrowed it from the girls' kendo club!" Yuigahama sounded awfully energetic, considering how she looked completely exhausted.

Yukinoshita twisted and stretched around to check her outfit, adjusting her collar. "Well then, let's get started," she said, walking out to the center of the dojo.

The audience, which had been watching all this happen, applauded Yukinoshita's dignified arrival.

Shiroyama, the judge, tilted his head in confusion. But when his eyes met mine, he turned pensive, then nodded. It seemed he interpreted this as "the show."

Uh, it's not, though...

For this second round, opposing Yukinoshita was once again the purple yam or sweet potato or whoever. Both competitors went to their positions and exchanged glances. Already, Yukinoshita had won on glare alone.

The flag was flown, and the judge cried, "Begin!"

Instantly, Yukinoshita's opponent snapped into action. He was fighting a girl, so he must have calculated that if he just got hold of her, he could use his strength to throw her.

But that would only work if his opponent were a regular girl.

Just who do you think you're up against? This is Yukino Yukinoshita. She has some of the best base stats in the prefecture, with superior ingenuity, strategy, valor, and beauty to go with a calm, collected, sharp, and vicious personality. By the way, she's also a perpetual winner and an extremely sore loser. In all competitions, she is, provisionally, the greatest.

She wouldn't let the rank and file even touch her.

And indeed, Yukinoshita didn't even let him touch her sleeves.

She read her opponent's breathing, predicting when he would step out from his inhalations. Then she simply reacted to these predictable actions with her optimal response. She danced around him with agility, redirecting her opponent like a matador.

And the direction she had designated for him was thin air.

Before he knew it, victory had already been decided.

There was a dramatic thud, and then the dojo was so silent I could even hear Yukinoshita's sigh.

The air was different. Not a single person in the audience made a sound.

Breaking the stillness was the flutter of the flag and the voice declaring her victory.

Having witnessed such a rare and excellent performance, the

audience welled with applause and cheers. Yukinoshita walked down the red carpet of their acclaim and returned to where we sat.

Yuigahama leaped up to glomp her. "Wow, wow! That was so cool!"

"Hey... You're suffocating me." Yukinoshita complained, but she didn't peel Yuigahama off. Even she couldn't dodge this.

The pair made for a pleasant sight, but the fact of the matter was that what Yukinoshita had just pulled off was less pleasant.

She threw someone just by dodging... What the hell, is she Kenichi's teacher? She had actually kicked that guy's butt without letting him lay a finger on her.

"You really are incredible," I said.

Yukinoshita smiled mischievously. "Oh, I suppose. Was that a little too much for an opening performance?"

"I don't think it's nice to be a bully."

Before going out into the ring, I stretched wide one last time. "Right, then. Let's go...," I muttered. I meant to talk to myself, but I got a reply.

"Come back safe!"

"Be good."

Are you guys my mom?

X X X

At last, the final match. With this, this ridiculously named S1 Grand Prix festival would be over.

The audience was already starting to thin.

Well, to be frank, this was superfluous. This was like an extra arc after the main story. The audience would have been fully satisfied by seeing Hayama's exploits, the dramatic interruption, and Yukinoshita's acrobatics, too.

That was why from here on out, I would do as I pleased. I'd planned out everything. So they would let me have this.

I went into the middle of the ring, and my opponent was about to approach. I'd already forgotten if I was facing Tsukui or Fujino or whoever, and I held up a hand to stop him. Then I called out to the head of the dojo. "How about it?"

He must not have expected I would seriously call him down, as he did a double take at me. We'd already broken the rule of changing the lineup in the last round. The rules didn't restrict us anymore.

The only thing holding him back would be shame.

He was embarrassed over being an outsider in the school, a real judo athlete being rounded up to this kind of game.

But if the needles pointed in the other direction, he'd be forced to join in.

He would be ashamed over not having the courage to come out when called onto the stage in a finals match in front of an excited audience.

Only he could know which would win over, but I was certain he would protect himself from the latter shame.

The audience was holding their collective breath, watching as the graduate pushed himself to his feet. Then he picked up his judo outfit and went to change.

That action caused the audience to give an expectant "Ohhhhh."

Meanwhile, Shiroyama, acting as judge, was expressionless. "... He's good."

"I'm sure. That's what'll make this final match exciting, right?" I replied as I checked my collar, sleeves, and belt, and Shiroyama tilted his head.

Shiroyama was sharper than you'd assume from his appearance. And that acuity would lead him to consider the meaning of what I'd just said. He was thoughtful enough to have explored the possibilities himself somewhat before coming to consult with us at the Service Club and had come to a reasonable decision. That was why I could expect that much from him.

But he wasn't much sharper than that. Even if he'd read into what I'd said, he wouldn't reach further into any deeper layers.

I'd made just one preparation. Well, it was something like insurance. It would be best if I could avoid using it.

The graduate was unsurprisingly used to slipping into his uniform, so he got changed quickly and came into the ring. He drove away the first-year with a hand, then approached the middle, facing off with me.

The eyes he had fixed on me were blazing with anger and humiliation. But I wouldn't lose on a glare. My perspective can make even the brightest light dull and murky.

This was how I could see the graduate well, too.

"Both competitors, bow. Begin!" Shiroyama commanded in his low voice.

Once it started, the graduate and I both inched in a bit, measuring the distance between us, advancing and retreating over and over. He didn't fiercely charge in. Of course, neither did I. Judo is all about falls. In class, about all I've been doing, to the best of my ability, has been falls, which I can practice by myself.

Day after day, falls.

I've mastered taking hits so well, rolling with the punches has become my whole life, really.

I knew full well that I'd never beat this guy legitimately. Even I'm not that full of myself. That was why I maintained a fixed distance as much as possible, always waiting for my moment of attack.

However, a master of technique will quickly see through an amateur's thoughts. Having realized that I was not going to attack, the graduate took a haughty step forward, breaking the balance in the space between us. By the time I was thinking *Oh no*, he'd already grabbed me, and he cut my pivot leg with a leg sweep from the outside.

I felt the floor come out from under me, and a shock ran through my back. An "...Ow" left my mouth. *What was that speed...? That was way beyond anything I could properly catch in a fall...*

The graduate must have been certain of his victory, as he was already returning to the start line.

The audience was sighing, too, starting to stand up.

That was why now would be my moment to attack. "Oh, you got me, man. Sweat is so slippery," I said, completely shamelessly.

Everyone was looking at me, like, *What the hell is this guy talking about?* That included the graduate, the audience, Yukinoshita, and

Yuigahama. Oh, I was thinking the same. There was no way an excuse like this could fly.

But it just had to work on one person.

The judge, Shiroyama, still had yet to raise the flag and had not yet made the call, either.

Noticing this, I added, "Just checking here—but tripping is invalid, right?"

Shiroyama was silent. Then he took a good look at my face and nodded. "Both competitors, return to the starting line."

Why? Because this was "the show."

The audience was indignant, and so was the graduate. "Come on," he pressed, "clearly that was a down! He didn't trip..." As he spoke, he looked at his feet. There remained the trail from when Zaimokuza had been towed away. In all the hullabaloo with Hayama and Yukinoshita, they'd forgotten to wipe it clean—despite how they'd wiped it properly after every match.

"But that was a point!" The graduate snapped at Shiroyama.

But that didn't change the decision. No—Shiroyama couldn't decide if it was okay to change the decision.

I don't know much about sports, but even I know that it's unusual for a misjudgment to be acknowledged—in student athletics, pro sports, or at a national-level tournament.

And, as the pièce de résistance, there was a rule to keep in mind: "Defying the judge disqualifies you, you know."

"What?" The graduate shifted his gaze from Shiroyama to me. He was like a raging beast. Frankly speaking, it was terrifying.

I quelled the tremble in my voice with a shrug of my shoulders. "That's what the world is like, right? It's harsh out there, isn't it?"

The graduate's expression turned bitter. As expected, he seemed aware he had a habit of saying that. He didn't have to tell me that he meant to crush me thoroughly this time.

"Both competitors, return to the starting line," Shiroyama said, taking control again, and the graduate reluctantly went back. But when we faced each other again, he glared at me with bloodshot eyes.

This was bad. This was very bad.

That cheat I'd just used for the sake of "the show" was only a one-time insurance. I couldn't use the same thing again. The audience wouldn't allow that, and my opponent definitely wouldn't. Most of all, Shiroyama wouldn't do it. The evidence for that was in the pallor of his face. This was quite a load of stress for him.

"Begin," Shiroyama called. His tone lacked its earlier strength.

In fact, even the audience's calls had petered out. Some had gotten bored and were leaving, too. That was why my panting breaths and the graduate's shouts were clearly audible.

And that was why he'd be able to hear me clearly when I spoke to him. "It's funny, isn't it?"

He'd probably never had someone speak to him in a match before, as he gave me a dubious look. The audience seemed to notice that I was talking, too, as I could sense their eyes and ears on us.

"I mean you got into university on a sports recommendation... It's surprising you still have the time to come check out the judo club here."

I saw his feet clearly stop in their tracks. "...Shut up. You don't know what you're talking about." His fists, lifting me up by the collar, clenched harder.

But he wasn't looking at me at all.

He was looking behind me, and to either side. At the audience.

They were murmuring, probably questioning why the match was suddenly in deadlock. Or maybe they were suspicious of what we were talking about. But regardless, from the graduate's position, he would feel that our conversation was creating the stir.

That was why I kept going, making an effort to stay calm and observe him so that I could respond to his movements. "Your club in university isn't a casual one, right? You're doing it for serious? You can only play around when you're in high school."

"Shut up." The graduate took an impulsive step inward, as if he meant to end the match quickly and stop me from talking any more.

I stepped back in equal proportion, maintaining a fixed distance. Then I gave him a nonchalant smile. "It really is a harsh world out there."

Just how many in the audience heard me?

The audience was clearly smaller than it was at the start of the match. But even this many was enough.

To be clear, it didn't matter if anyone actually heard us or not. It was enough for him to worry that some people might be.

"It really is like you said. That's why you came back here, isn't it?"

"..." With that, I'd silenced him—with his own words.

And now I had accomplished my goal: denunciation before an audience. To damage his dignity, his pride as their senior. To make this graduate think that a crowd of students had heard me. Whether they'd actually heard it wasn't the issue. I just had to make him question if he was capable of showing his face to society.

It frankly didn't matter who won or lost after that.

The fact was that his eyes had been darting around for a while now. He was rattled, focused on what the people around him thought of him.

I could clearly see his spirit breaking down. The signs had been there from the start. I'd gotten a hunch back when I'd first heard about him.

Glorification of the past is proof of a weakened heart.

The desire to talk about bygone glory is evidence of a spirit grown old.

That graduate had probably experienced failure at university. He'd lost his confidence, pride, and everything that went with it, and that was what had sent him running back here.

He may not have been aware of what he was doing. Maybe he'd come by on a whim, found it surprisingly comfortable, and then he'd just stuck around.

But that didn't mean it was okay for him to be here. For the people below, those who descend back down from on high are a nuisance. The world doesn't have the time to take care of those who come running back.

That was why I would drive him out. Expel him. Eject him.

Oh, it's exactly like you said: The world is harsh.

The graduate was biting his lip. His grip on my sleeve had already weakened.

He probably wouldn't come anymore. A fugitive has to keep running.

But if I was to make absolutely sure…

…then it would be best to win.

The ultimate humiliation of losing to an amateur like me in front of an audience would break his spirit completely.

And so I hammered in the final lynchpin. "You didn't come back here. You ran away from there."

It seemed I'd managed to pull that final trigger. The graduate reacted as if he'd been struck.

So now was the time to do it. I pulled at his sleeve, an invitation. It tricked him easily. Where he'd been slack before, he was now firmly tensed. Had I succeeded in provoking him?

He came for me.

I didn't dodge.

I was conscious of every point of balance.

I'd been through class, and I'd felt his throw just now, so I understood the form. Guess getting thrown around does count as practice. I made up for my inept technique with extra force.

I just had to manipulate him into a position where I could throw him. I focused all my strength on that endeavor alone. I showed no other resistance and just left it to the gravity of the earth, the law of inertia, and fighting instinct.

I got him over my shoulder, and then from behind me, I heard him say, his tone both harsh and also somewhat calm, "Shut up. I know all that."

And then there was only the fall.

Without a moment's delay, the flag went up.

I could hear the audience applauding the victory, echoing loud in the dojo.

"Point! Match over!" This cry was, more than any I'd heard from Shiroyama, the most perfectly clear and beautiful.

By contrast, someone else's voice was dull and pathetic.

"…Ow."

X X X

The remaining time before summer vacation sped by like a whirlwind, and a few days later, my heart was dancing with summer vacation finally within reach.

So even though I didn't really want to be in the Service Club room, I came in humming.

A few more sleeps, and it'd be summer vacation. The dillydallying of the days ahead was waiting for me.

When I opened the door of the clubroom, as usual, Yukinoshita was reading a book by the window, and Yuigahama was facedown on her desk like a dog, on her phone. I took one last look at this scene.

"Hey," I greeted them casually, then sat down on a diagonal from Yukinoshita, in the most distant seat.

She looked up from her paperback. "My, is your back better already?"

"Nope. But it got me out of gym class," I replied.

And now Yuigahama raised her head. "Judo, right? How admirable of you to keep your promise."

"Nothing admirable about it. It was just the silver lining."

At the very end of the judo tournament, that graduate had thrown me down hard. Rubbing my creaking, injured back, I'd been forced to make a promise as the loser.

That promise was to never get involved with the judo club ever again. Yuigahama and Yukinoshita had both been very angry about my attitude, railing on at me about how I was a bad influence on the members and had been disrespecting judo and stuff. And so the dream of becoming an Olympic gold medalist in judo had been stolen from me before I ever even thought to have it.

Well, with my back in this state, I doubt I could do judo even if I wanted to try. It really hurt, and all night I'd been muttering as much.

It still hurt, but since I got to sit on the sidelines in gym for a while, the pros and cons balanced out... Actually, I get the feeling there were clearly more cons. Was I this bad at arithmetic?

"Well, it's good that was all you got," said Yukinoshita. "You should be thankful to Shiroyama."

"Yeah, yeah. That guy was glaring at you so hard it looked like he was gonna kill you, Hikki." Yuigahama agreed.

And that made me think back. "Hmm, Shiroyama, huh?" I hadn't even spoken to Pota-yama-slash-Shiroyama since then.

This was partly because I'd been forced into making that weird promise to the graduate. But, well, both of us were tiptoeing around each other. And I don't do a lot of tiptoeing, so this was quite the event. Yeah, I'll admit I kinda forced him into a cruel position. The greatest kindness I could offer him would be to ensure we never interact so he wouldn't suffer any further.

"So what's gone on with the judo club since then?" I asked. Of course, with the *geas* cast on me preventing me from being involved with them again, there was no way for me to know.

Unsurprisingly, Yuigahama was well connected and informed. She *clackity-clack*ed into her cell phone, probably texting someone about it. "Um, well, they haven't really gotten any more new members, but they say a bunch of the guys who quit have come back."

"Oh?" Well, if a demonstration like that would get new people to join, no club would ever struggle. And that's not even touching on how the biggest stars of that event had been Hayama, Zaimokuza, and Yukinoshita. There wasn't much that would have inspired people to join the judo club, as an organization.

"It wasn't quite all of them, but some former members came back because that graduate stopped coming," Yukinoshita supplemented as she turned the page of her paperback.

"Oh yeah. That's surprising, huh? He did win in the end, so you'd think he'd be all, *I'm the strongest! Augh!* And come more."

"Uh, I don't think so," I remarked, snickering at Yuigahama's ditzy gesticulating.

Yukinoshita seemed to find fault with this, as she dropped her bookmark into her paperback and closed it with a smack. "I don't suppose you figured this would happen and lost deliberately?"

"Uh, I did pretty seriously go in to win…" In fact, I'd even thought I had won there at the end.

"…Wow, that's sad."

No need to be quite so honest, okay, Miss Yuigahama?

"Is that right…? It looked to me as if you were provoking him. I thought for sure your plan was to cede victory to accomplish some greater end."

Yukinoshita had the habit of thinking too much about things, but I could see where she was coming from.

"It didn't matter if I won or lost; that's all. But if I *had* won, then the guy would've been more likely to stop coming."

"What do you mean?" Yuigahama's eyebrows quirked upward thoughtfully as she considered with a *hmm*.

But it wasn't that complex. "Nothing much. All I had to do was teach him how 'there's no seat for your ass anyway!'" I said.

But that just made Yuigahama's eyebrows even more confused. My point had not been communicated.

Yukinoshita, however, cracked a smile. "…I see," she replied. Just that one remark, as if she understood, then she returned to her reading.

The gesture piqued Yuigahama's curiosity, and she went over to shake the answer out of Yukinoshita. "Huh? What's that mean? What's that mean?"

Yukinoshita looked extremely annoyed at being rattled around, but she was stubbornly committed to reading. It looked like the pair would be fooling around for a little while more.

Like Yukinoshita, I pulled a book out of my bag and opened up to my bookmarked page. But even when I ran my eyes across the lines, my head didn't really absorb the content, and I gave up and closed it again.

That graduate must have seen this school as the place he wanted to come back to. It had made him feel nostalgic, comfortable, and glad—so much so that he'd heedlessly wanted to make it his escape.

But his escape here had trapped him even further. So with that stress on his shoulders, he'd wanted to run even further—an endless loop of running from reality. That was why, unless he saw himself in the mirror and felt the gaze of society and the light of day, he wouldn't have even been able to recognize that fact.

In the end, if you generate stress for yourself, you're the only one who can relieve it. You either keep running, or you turn around and face it. Which option did that graduate choose?

Well, it didn't matter. His final remark to me at the end of the match still echoed in my ears.

I looked out the window.

Big, billowing columns of clouds rose up over the distant line of the horizon over the sea. I could hear the yells of the sports clubs, the tones of the brass band, and the lively voices of the girls' chattering filling the clubroom.

Suddenly, I wondered.

One day, would I have a place that I wanted to go back to?

The question stayed in my mind.

Short Story 4
Regardless, **Hachiman Hikigaya**'s positive thinking is completely twisted.

It was now the time of cool breezes—or rather, winds that occasionally ran cold.

"The Chiba Prefecture–Wide Advice E-mail..." I announced the title as listlessly as the stirring fall wind, and Yuigahama gave a patter of applause. But then Yukinoshita gave her a dubious glance, and the applause wilted away.

Yuigahama pulled herself together, opened the inbox, and started reading the first e-mail. "Umm, the first message of the day is from Chiba city, username: Master Swordsman General."

Request for advice from username: Master Swordsman General
A deadline for one of the biggest imprints in the industry is nigh. Victory, how?!

...He sends way too many of these. He's scary, like someone aggressively trying to talk to a bot on Twitter.

"What is this?" Having read the e-mail, Yuigahama tilted her head, and with a sigh, Yukinoshita summoned me.

"Hikigaya."

"I know, I know."

At this point it's like—like taking care of your aging parents. It's fine; I'll stay with you until the end… Having attained this state of benevolence—of sheer enlightenment—I typed out an e-mail.

Response from the Service Club:
Don't give me this selfish stuff about the biggest in the business. Just send it in to Gagaga Bunko. It'll be fine; they're with Showgakkan (or whatever they're called). Also, as a Gagaga author, it seems you will not be able to marry a voice actress.

"Well, that's one down. Next, Yuigahama." Despite not having done anything, Yukinoshita wore an expression of relief as she prompted the next.

Not even questioning it, Yuigahama started reading out the next e-mail. "Um, next message. In Chiba city, from the username: Bro's little sister."

Request for advice from username: Bro's little sister
    Maybe it's 'cause it's been cold lately, but the cat's been coming into bed with me, and he uses my arm as his pillow. I've never even done that with my bro! (That was worth a lot of Komachi points.) Komachi can't roll over, and he keeps huffing right in my ear. It's kind of annoying. Is there a good way to deal with this?

Once Yuigahama was finished reading it out, both girls gave me strangely unenthusiastic looks.

"So she says, Bro."

"There you have it, Bro."

"Shut up. And don't call me Bro." Komachi is the only one allowed to call me that. If they say *Bro Bro* too much, I'll go and found Chanko Dining or something.

"…By the way, ah, does your cat actually, um, sleep together with you? A-and sleep on your arm?" Yukinoshita glanced over at me, eyes upturned like she was somehow embarrassed. It was a sweet gesture, but unfortunately, her tightly clenched fists robbed it of any cuteness.

"No. With me, that cat always comes straight on top of my stomach," I said, and Yuigahama laughed at me.

"Doesn't that mean he's treating you with contempt? Kamakura sees you as beneath him, Hikki."

"He's not like your dog."

"Cats are fundamentally solitary creatures, so they don't have a social hierarchy. They will form groups, but in their case, it appears to be closer to a parent-child relationship. It may be that with Komachi, he's displaying the sort of dependent behavior he would show toward a mother cat." Yukinoshita expertly rattled off an analysis-filled something or other... Yuigahama and I were both kinda weirded out.

"You know everything, huh, Yukipedia...?"

"Would you stop calling me that?" Yukinoshita glared at me sullenly. It seemed she was not as all-knowing as a certain other -pedia. Well, if she didn't like it, it was best to revise that form of address.

"Sorry, Catipedia."

"There you go."

"You're okay with *that*?!"

It seemed she was, as Yukinoshita ignored Yuigahama's surprise and gave a satisfied nod.

Thanks to Yukinoshita's pointless lecture, I basically understood what my cat was doing. "...In other words, you're saying he climbs onto my stomach because of my overflowing househusband aura." Even cats recognize that I was made to be a househusband. I'd expect nothing less of myself. I believe I'd like to live a catlike lifestyle in the future.

But Yukinoshita's lips twitched in a cold smile, ready to destroy my ambition. "Couldn't you also say that a cat sitting on you is similar to a feline parent holding its kitten?"

"So he's being treated like a kid."

"...Heh, so, like, my overflowing dependent aura is what makes him do that." I even made a cat want to support me. Wow, me.

"That's some serious positive thinking!"

"We've gone beyond positive thinking at this point; it's down-right mania… Well, maybe there's something to be learned from such a perspective," Yukinoshita commented, then began typing a response e-mail.

```
Response from the Service Club:
You get to sleep with a cat. You can put up with a
few annoyances, can't you?
```

Just get a cat already.

Afterword

Hello, this is Wataru Watari.

Out in the world, summer vacation is already in full swing. Where's my break?

So summer vacation is a wonderful season for making lots of memories, but once you're an adult looking back, memories are not at all limited to special events. A lot of them are just trivial mundane things that stick oddly in your head.

I'm sure it just feels that way because if something happens on a day-to-day basis, it's labeled as mundane, but to the person who's living it, it might be something more special. It's common to downplay the importance of something like a love affair, a personal relationship, or a nice meal, to see it as just one of the common sights of life, but to the person in question, it can be a major, life-changing thing.

And so this time around, I've brought to you a collection of short stories.

Now then, speaking of the mundane and the uncommon, the uncommon has become the mundane for me lately. What the heck, why is my life like a light novel now? However, I have not met anyone.

And now, the acknowledgments.

Holy Ponkan8: Hey? Clearly, Miura's the heroine, okay? This Miura cover I wanted so bad was so cute, it scared me. This one was the best, yet again! You did a great job! Thank you so much.

To my editor, Hoshino: You put so much effort not only into the editing of this book but also into the multimedia-related work, too. This hell march will continue. This death parade will go on and on. And so thank you very much for your efforts.

To everyone involved in the multimedia franchise, including the anime staff and cast: Thanks to you, we've made it through the airing of the TV anime. I know I've caused a lot of trouble, but I'm really grateful that it came together. Thank you very much.

And to all my readers: Thank you very much for all your great support for all the multimedia works in this series, including the books and TV anime. I'm really glad that your support has enabled us to put it out into the world. From now on, we will continue to build on it bit by bit. I hope you will continue to stick with me.

And around here is where I run out of pages, so here I will lay down my pen.

Right, then. Let's meet again in Volume 8!

On a certain day in July, in a certain place in Chiba, while preparing to go buy MAX Coffee in the middle of the night,

Wataru Watari

Translation
Notes

SS1 ⋯ **Hachiman Hikigaya**'s idea of "Mom's cooking" is wrong, as I expected.

P. 5 "**I may have M-2 syndrome, but I want to be in love**" is the more direct translation of the title of the light-novel series *Love, Chunibyo & Other Delusions.*

P. 7 "**The two of them looked ready to nuke me to Neo Tokyo.**" Tokyo being nuked to create Neo Tokyo is part of the premise of *Akira*. The Japanese line here is a rather untranslatable pun: "I'd thoroughly exasperated them. Which makes me think, if you write *exasperated* (*akire* in Japanese) as *AKIRE*, it really sounds like a certain well-known movie (referring to the film *Akira*)."

SA A ⋯ We must wish **them all** the best in their futures.

P. 13 "**…buy some gargling solution and come home to a hippo.**" This is a reference to a 1995 ad for Isodine (*isojin*), a gargling solution to prevent sickness. A woman comes home, saying, "There's no one here to welcome me home…" She's greeted by a couple of miniature hippos (mascots for the brand), and they gargle together.

P. 14   **"Pretty American. Or Nagoyan. Looks good, meow."** This is a call-back to a few jokes Hachiman made in Volume 7, chapter 8, about breakfast sets popular in Nagoya, and Nagoya dialect making it sound like they're meowing at the end of their sentences.

P. 14   **"…for your bacon—I learned that from *Silver Spoon*."** *Silver Spoon* is a manga/anime about farming, and being thankful to the animals that provide the meat you eat is a big theme of the series.

P. 14   **"…can't forget to say thank you, my twilight…"** The original Japanese gag here was a reference to the Arashi song "Kansha Kangeki Amearashi," itself a wordplay on an overwrought way of saying thank you. "Thank You, My Twilight" is the name of a song by the Pillows that features in several episodes of *FLCL Progressive* and *FLCL Alternative*.

P. 16   **"Are you a mayo maniac? Or a Shino-maniac? That's ultra-relaxing."** The terms (*mayolar* and *Shinolar*) sound more similar in Japanese. A *mayolar* is someone who puts mayonnaise on everything, while *Shinolar* refers to a late 1990s fashion trend of imitating the brightly colored, eclectic style of the celebrity Tomoe Shinohara. "Ultra Relax" was the title of her 1997 single and the opening song for the anime *Kodomo no Omocha* (published in English as *Kodocha: Sana's Stage*).

P. 17   **"Why's it named like that magical girl show?"** Hikigaya is referring to the 1990s magical girl anime *Wedding Peach*.

P. 17   **"Dreamin'"** is the name of a song by BOOWY, notable only in that it has a lot of Engrish, much like the title of this magazine in Japanese.

P. 22   **"…going around to each and every person, asking, *Will you wind? Yes/no.*"** This is a reference to the manga *Rozen Maiden*, in which the protagonist receives a letter asking him this question, in reference to whether he will wind up a clockwork doll.

P. 28 **Sachi Usuko** (literally meaning "unlucky girl") is a character played by a member of the pop idol group Morning Musume on the variety show *Hello!*

P. 30 **Bride training** (*hanayome shuugyou*) refers to a woman practicing cooking, cleaning, and other domestic tasks in preparation for marriage. Cooking is generally the dominant task on the list.

P. 30 **"The heart-fluttering brideness showdown~! ♪"** Heart-fluttering showdown (*dokidoki taiketsu*) refers to a gag from the manga *Uchuu no Housoku Sekai no Kihon* (Laws of the universe, fundamentals of the world) by Toraichiro Ota. It's basically just an excuse to talk about the author's taste in women.

P. 31 **"*Hammerspace? Really?*"** The original line was "Come on, are you some BØY?" in reference to the manga *Hareluya II Boy* by Haruto Umezawa. The protagonist will pull various implements out of thin air from behind his back, usually baseball bats and frying pans.

P. 32 **"Oh, no, no, no! Yoshi-*no* Nanjou!"** Yoshino Nanjou is a voice actress and singer.

P. 33 *Battlefield Baseball* (*Jigoku Koshien*) is a gag manga with a film adaptation that skewers high school sports by turning it into a horror-style blood-and-gore fest.

P. 35 **Saize** (Saizeriya) is a cheap Japanese-style Italian restaurant chain.

P. 42 **"My recommendation there is *The Little Prince*. Okay, then I'll cover both bases and go with *The Prince of Tennis!*"** Hachiman is just referring back to Totsuka's role in their class play. *The Prince of Tennis* is a sports manga and has nothing to do with actual princes of any sort, though its longtime popularity among *fujoshi* for BL reasons does lend an extra layer to this reference.

P. 43   *Hinedere* is a word Komachi makes up to describe Hachiman in Volume 4, riffing off terms like *tsundere*. It's a combination of *twisted* and *lovestruck*.

P. 50   *KanColle* is the abbreviated name of *Kantai Collection*, a web browser game featuring warships personified as girls.

Bonus track! "Komachi Hikigaya's Plot."

P. 63   *Ryojin Hisho* (Songs to make the dust dance on the beams) is a collection of songs popular in twelfth-century Japan.

P. 64   **Emperor Go-Shirakawa** was the emperor from around the time *Ryojin Hisho* was written, during the Heian period.

P. 64   **"...a Gadabout can change classes to Sage at level 20."** This is a reference to *Dragon Quest III*.

P. 64   *Enka* is a popular musical form made to resemble traditional Japanese music stylistically. Melancholy, sentimental ballads about heartbreak are a staple. It's considered rather old-fashioned.

P. 66   **"PaRappa"** refers to the PS1-era rhythm game *PaRappa the Rapper*. It's not really relevant; the name just sounds sort of like Doppler.

P. 66   **"Bravery is our birthright, lads!"** is a quote from Will Zepelli in *JoJo's Bizarre Adventure*.

P. 68   *No Longer Human* by Osamu Dazai is one of the most well-known works of contemporary Japanese literature and deals with the subject of societal alienation, among other things.

P. 69   *"These girlish lovers are a sight to behold, like a golden mosaic."* *Girlish Lover* is the name of the OP for *Oreshura* (*My Girlfriend and My Childhood Friend Fight Too Much*), and *Kiniro Mosaic* (*Golden Mosaic*) is a four-panel gag comic series. The former is a harem show, and the latter is a cute girls / slice of life manga, so they're not really relevant in terms of content; this gag is a title reference.

P. 69   **"And then yet another white lily jumped into this *yuri*-licious scene."** A white lily, or *yuri*, is code for girl/girl manga.

P. 72   **"Despairingly cool!"** is the line that comes during the next-episode previews of *Chousoku Henkei Gyrozetter* (Super high-speed transforming Gyrozetter). It's about transforming robots.

P. 73   **"Hachiman knows. All of Class 2-F are good friends! Except me."** This is in reference to an Internet meme. The original is "Moppii knows all about that. Moppii knows everyone loves her." Created by 2ch, Moppii is a cute blob character, a "witch who watches over threads regarding sales of anime products." She was originally based on the character Houki Shinonono from the Infinite Stratos series, but she took on a life of her own as a meme.

P. 74   *Purikura* is short for "print club." They are photo booths equipped with various filters to make your skin whiter, eyes larger, and legs longer and add all sorts of digital effects before the photos are printed.

P. 75   **"...those people who don't have enough friends to make a collection, or those who try to turn over a new leaf and still end up living in a tent..."** Referencing the games *Friends Collection* and *Animal Crossing: New Leaf.*

P. 75   **"...Haruno would be loved by the tiles..."** Being "loved by the tiles" is a characteristic of the titular character in the mah-jongg manga *Saki.*

P. 75   **"...Kawa-something seems like she'd be supergood at digital style."** "Digital style" is the mah-jongg play style of Nodoka Haramura, also from *Saki.*

P. 76   **"...throwing uncensored porn at a cute girl who still believes in cabbage patches and storks."** This is a reference to a line from the character Itsuki in *Yu Yu Hakusho*.

P. 76   **"I can go out in mah-jongg, but not on a date... Ha-ha-ha...hah..."** "Going out" in mah-jongg means getting rid of all your tiles, or losing the game. This is adapted from the Japanese wordplay *"pon kan shin,"* where *pon* and *kan* are mah-jongg terms (pong and chow) and *kanshin* means "interest."

P. 82   **"*Quiz Magic Chibademy!*"** This is riffing off *Quiz Magic Academy*, the long-running series of arcade quiz games.

P. 84   The **Ostrich Kingdom** is an ostrich farm and general tourist attraction located in Chiba.

P. 84   **Chiiba-kun** is a red dog and the mascot character for Chiba prefecture. His body is shaped like the borders of Chiba.

P. 85   *Fastest Finger First* is a manga about a high school quiz-bowl club.

P. 86   **"You've got guts, little firefighter."** This quote is from the manga *Firefighter! Daigo of Company M* by Masahito Soda. As a child, the protagonist runs back into a burning building to save a dog, and the firefighter who rescues him says that line to him, inspiring him to become a firefighter.

P. 89   **"Hammer chance"** is a card in the WIXOSS TCG that can only be used when your life is at zero. Basically, it's a chance at a comeback.

P. 92   **"What the heck, is this some Chiba anime?"** This refers to *Oreimo* (*There's No Way My Little Sister Could Be This Cute*), which is set in Chiba.

P. 92   **Zero Requiem** is Lelouch's plan in *Code Geass* to end all war and usher in an age of peace.

SS3 ··· Unexpectedly, **Hachiman Hikigaya**'s studying methods are not wrong.

P. 100   **Gagaga Bunko** is the imprint that publishes this series in Japanese.

SA B ··· **They** have yet to know of a place they should go back to.

P. 108   **"Barf Spark–level obnoxious."** Barf Spark is meme from the Touhou Project games, relating specifically to *yukkuris* (disembodied character heads) and a method by which *yukkuris* brutally kill one another.

P. 108   **"Japan's summer is not Kincho's summer."** This is an advertising slogan for a brand of insect repellent.

P. 109   **"…some bullshit I'd learned from *Rurouni Kenshin*…"** The manga *Rurouni Kenshin*, which is about a Meiji-period swordsman, features the "formless stance," a staple of Kenshin's flexible fighting style.

P. 109   The **Tenchi-matou stance** is the ultimate stance used by Vearn, the villain of the manga *Dragon Quest: The Adventure of Dai*. It's supposed to counter any and all attacks.

P. 109   **"…get the wind to blow my hair back like T.M.Revolution…"** TMR is a pop artist with a long history of doing anime and game theme songs. He's done a few videos that involve getting buffeted by the elements, including "High Pressure," "White Breath," and "Hot Limit," making "pretending to be TMR" into a meme.

P. 109   **"Ah, My Angel Totsuka. I want to answer quiz questions right to make him grow."** This is a reference to a series of quiz arcade games called Kosodate Quiz: My Angel (Parenting quiz: My angel) in which the parent has to successfully answer questions to raise their daughter's age from zero to twenty-five years old.

P. 110   **Black Jack** is an unlicensed physician and the protagonist of the manga *Black Jack* by Osamu Tezuka.

P. 111 "**Whichever the case, if it were *Another*, you'd be dead.**" This line is a meme that originated with the series of mystery horror novels and their anime adaptation. The series involves a lot of gruesome deaths.

P. 112 "**...the 'I'm a *satorare* theory.'**" *Satorare* is a fictional ailment that causes the sufferer's feelings to be projected as waves and transmitted to people around them. Originates from the manga *Satorare* by Makoto Satou.

P. 116 "**...Everyone is the same, and everyone is good.**" This is a deliberate misquoting of Misuzu Kaneko, the early twentieth-century poet. The actual line from her poem "Me, a Birdie and a Bell" is "Everyone is different, and everyone is good."

P. 117 "**Personally, I like to keep the summer humidity at bay with my dry sense of humor.**" The original line here is "Oh God, why have you made me think about this nonsense?" The Japanese pun was on *kami* (hair), *kami* (paper), and *kami* (god).

P. 117 "**When droplets of sweat hit the paper, the way it goes all limp can be a real mood-killer.**" The original Japanese contains a reference to a gay porn called *A Midsummer Night's Lewd Dream* that ended up becoming memeified.

P. 119 "*She's kinda making it out to be like Trouble Contractors, or TRO-CON, for short. Is there gonna be a coconut crab massacre?*" Trouble Contractor is the profession of the protagonist of *Lost Universe*, a series of light novels by Hajime Kanzaka from the 1990s that also have an anime adaptation. The "coconut crab massacre" is the name of the infamous fourth episode, which is known for being a poorly animated mess with loads of production issues.

P. 130, 131 "*There's no seat for your ass anyway!*" This is a line from Midori Iwamoto in the J-drama *Life*. She says it to her former "bad friend"

Manami Anzai, when she dumps her graffiti-tagged desk and chair out the classroom window.

P. 132 **CoCoICHI** is Coco Ichibanya (a curry restaurant), while **Karekichi** is another curry restaurant.

P. 132 *"…this* inkare *thing sounds like a topic a certain curry-loving voice actor would enjoy."* Hachiman's voice actor in the anime, Takuya Eguchi, is a famous curry maniac.

P. 146 **"Herk! A competition?!"** In Japanese, this cry is *hoge*, the wail of Kankichi, the protagonist of the long-running comedy manga *Kochikame* (the common abbreviation for the manga This is the police station in front of Kameari Park in Katsushika Ward).

P. 146 **"No, I know thou lieth…"** In the original Japanese, the sentence ended here with *desushi osushi*, a sentence-ending particle popularized by players of the MMO *Final Fantasy XI*, combining the verbal tic *desushi* with a popular in-game item, *osushi*.

P. 148 *"I'm not wearing a construction helmet or anything, though. Maybe I should get fatter and fuzzier."* This is referring to the character Boss (Taishou-kun) in the anime *Hamtaro*. In Japanese, the reference is to his verbal quirk *dajee*.

P. 153 **Yamcha** is a character in the Dragon Ball series who gets thoroughly overshadowed by more powerful fighters who appear later in the series.

P. 155 **"Chii is learning"** became an Internet meme due to how often the robot girl says that line in the CLAMP manga and anime series *Chobits*. It's something said whenever you learn something new, especially new words.

P. 155 **"My ghost is whispering to me..."** is something Motoko Kusanagi says more than once in the anime *Ghost in the Shell*. *Ghost* here refers to the soul.

P. 161 **"*What the hell, is she Kenichi's teacher?*"** Hachiman is referencing the martial arts manga *Kenichi: the Mightiest Disciple*.

SS4 ⋯ Regardless, **Hachiman Hikigaya**'s positive thinking is completely twisted.

P. 174 **"If they say *Bro Bro* too much, I'll go and found Chanko Dining or something."** Chanko Dining is the name of a chain of restaurants founded by celebrity and former sumo wrestler Masaru Hanada. In his sumo wrestler days, he was known by the nickname Oniichan (big brother).